Lo

J.S. Ellis

For information contact:

Black Cat Ink Press

https://blackcatinkpress.com/

J.S Ellis

https://www.joannewritesbooks.com

Cover Design by Getcovers

Paperback: 978-99957-1-987-6

This book is written, edited and proofread in British English

Chapter One

'Phoebe, wake up!'

I heard a grunt which was coming from me. I snuggled into the duvet. It was still dark outside and I wanted to stay in bed a little longer. My bedroom door opened and Adele appeared.

'Don't you have classes today?' she asked.

'I do,' I groaned and buried my face in the pillow.

'I made you a cup of coffee. Up or you're going to be late.' Adele instructed.

'I hate January.'

'You said the same thing about December,' Adele laughed. 'Come on.' She went over to the window and opened the curtains and the light burst into the room, making me shut my eyes.

Adele and I were childhood friends. Our parents were neighbours, we went to the same schools and now we're in the same university, not taking the same classes together but we share a flat. Adele was an only child. I have a brother who's five years older than me, his name is Tom. Adele and I couldn't be more different. Adele had wavy blonde hair, which gives her that tousled look. Blue-green heavy-hooded eyes, and full cheekbones. I had straight black hair that falls like a glossy sheet to my back. Large brown, almond-shaped eyes, thick eyebrows, and plump lips which Adele described as "perfect for lipstick". It was the first time living with someone, and you learn more about a person when living with them. You get to know about their habits, their quirks, what makes them tick. Adele was messy and disorganised. There were pieces of clothing all over the apartment, on the floor, sofa, and armchair. When Adele wanted a drink, she never used the same glass but took out a fresh one and never washed it, which irritated the hell out of me, as there will be no clean glasses for me to drink from. Adele did the dusting, and strangely enough, loved to iron clothes. For someone so messy, it was a surprising quality. Adele said it relaxed her and I couldn't complain when I could watch TV while I had someone else ironing my shirts. Adele wasn't one for sauces, so this was my duty. Adele washed the bath, but if there were bits of my hair, I had to remove them. Which was more than fair.

I dragged my sleepy self out of bed and had a shower. Afterwards, I got dressed in a black turtleneck, mum's jeans, and trainers. My usual look. Comfortable and practical. I applied mascara on my eyelashes and blusher on my cheeks. Adele sat on a stool by the stainless kitchen counter, tapping on her phone and smiling mischievously. That smile, I knew too well. A smile that showed there was a guy involved. I didn't ask Adele who she was texting, nor if there was a bloke in the picture, she would tell me in her own time as Adele always did. We were both single, taking time off men. Well, Adele was taking time off from men, I didn't attract attention as she did. Adele had that bubbly, flirtatious attitude that made her irresistible to men. I was rather detached, aloof, hardly ever smiled, and sarcastic. So yes, we were different.

'I have English Lit,' she said through her texting and rolled her eyes.

We were to graduate that year if we passed our finals. Adele in English literature, me in finance. I had my life all planned out. After I graduated, I'd find a job in a big company, and learn all the ropes. Once I settled, I'd rent out a place of my own. Something big, more accommodating preferably, with a view of the Thames. Not that there was anything wrong with this apartment. It was big enough with two bedrooms, a kitchen, a living room where the black leather sofa sat in front of the TV. Nothing grand, no works of art, we couldn't afford that. Just cheap picture frames bought from Ikea. All the furnishings were from there; from the hickory furniture to the rugs on the floor.

Anyway, I fantasised about coming home after a tiresome day to find clean glasses and no clothes lying all over the place. I'd carefully laid my plan out, with the boxes ready to be ticked. I knew I would get there. In this perfectly planned life, I would picture a man, not just any man but *him*. My eyes moved to the window where our neighbour lives. My Alan. Well, he wasn't mine. He wasn't my boyfriend or anything like that. I'd never talked to the guy. I didn't think he was aware I existed. Adele told me his name. She had her way of finding out this kind of information. Alan lived across the street in the more sophisticated looking block. My bedroom had the perfect view of his bedroom, and I liked to watch him. Not in a creepy, *I am watching you* sort of way, but admiringly from a distance.

He was by far the most attractive man I ever laid my eyes on. I mean, what a guy. The first time I had seen him, I was on my way to the apartment and he stepped out from his block. He wore a green shirt under a leather biker jacket and jeans. Simple and classic. Compact. His sense of style didn't scream fashion-obsessed, quite the opposite, stylish but didn't give a damn. Cool. He was a sight to behold, way out of my league, but I couldn't help myself and there was no harm in looking. He was new, wrapped so prettily and delivered to me like a Christmas present. It was love at first sight, on my part. His hair was styled and greased like James Dean. His hair was brown with a touch of auburn, and he had blue eyes and sharp cheekbones. I presumed he was the same age as Tom, in his mid-twenties. I was a girl with a massive crush, but I did nothing about it. Adele knew, of course, and used to tease me about it. Her eyes flickered to the window, then turned her attention back to the phone.

'I'm going out tonight,' Adele announced.

'Okay,' I said.

'I'll be late.'

'It's fine.'

We took the bus to the university as usual. Adele had her earbuds on, deep in thought. We were comfortable in our silence, in our familiarity. Adele had a smile on her face, which she couldn't seem to wipe off. I knew that smile all too well. It was the kind that announced there was a lad involved and tonight, she was going to meet him. I made a mental note to call my parents.

We walked to the university gate where Hannah and Janice sat under a tree. Hannah held her phone and both were looking at it, smiling. They were Adele's friends. Although Adele and I had been friends for ages, Hannah and Janice weren't my sort of crowd. I wasn't a party girl, obsessed with the latest makeup or hair trend. It seemed so lame to me, but this was what they were into. Who was I to judge? They did their thing while I did mine.

'Hello, bitches,' Adele said.

Hannah and Janice snapped to attention.

'Adele!' both Hannah and Janice squeaked as if it had been ages since they had seen her.

'I hope you're not taking any selfies without me,' Adele warned.

The three of them posed with Adele's phone as they pressed their lip-glossed lips together and snapped the photo and filtered the shit out of it before posting it to Instagram or Facebook. They asked me to join them, but I wasn't interested. As I looked around me, everyone seemed so young, immature, and innocent. While I felt much older. I always felt that way I didn't know why.

Hannah was a voluptuous brunette and Janice was straw blonde with large round blue eyes.

'Want to join us tonight?' Hannah asked Adele.

Adele hesitated, 'No, I made plans.'

'Really, with who?' Hannah asked.

'I rather not tell,' Adele said in a sing-song voice.

They both gushed and I rolled my eyes.

'You have a date?' Janice said.

'Maybe.'

'Tell us everything,' Hannah said.

Janice turned to me, 'What about you? Want to join? We're ordering pizza and relaxing with Netflix.'

'Thanks, but I got to study,' I said.

A safe card to play.

And study I did. My desk was cluttered with books and notes. It was nearly midnight and Adele wasn't in yet. I didn't know how she did it. Stay out till the early hours of the morning and be fresh for classes the next day. I couldn't do it, I was more composed, more conscious, driven to succeed and do well for myself.

I rubbed my eyes and stood from my desk. The only sound in the apartment was coming from the cuckoo clock in the living room. I strolled to the kitchen and poured myself a glass of water and took it with me to the bedroom. I surveyed my desk with dispassion. Maybe, I could just sleep and continue tomorrow, I thought. I closed my books and tidied my desk. When I was done, I took a sip of water, getting ready for bed but first things first. I parted the curtain and his window came into view. He was there, but not alone. There was a girl with him. I gasped, she was only dressed if I could call it that, in matching white bra and knickers. Alan was fully dressed. Her long blonde hair concealed her face so I couldn't see her properly. I closed the curtain and stared at it in dismay as my heart thumped in my chest. It hadn't occurred to me that Alan had a girlfriend. He had moved in about five months ago and I'd never seen him with a woman. A guy that gorgeous wouldn't remain single for long. A woman had to come along and steal him away. I parted the curtain again. The woman had her back to him and he was planting kisses on her neck. His hands glided to her shoulder easing down the strap of her bra, planting more kisses there between her shoulder and neck and her face came to view.

I slammed my eyes shut and opened them again as if my own eyes were betraying me. *It couldn't be.* My body went stiff. I wanted to move from the window, shut the curtain and digest all of this but my feet were paralysed, forcing me to stand there and take it. I parted my lips as a wave of hurt slashed through me. Adele with *him!* How predictable. We might have been friends, but it was typical of Adele to do something like this. Waves of anger replaced the hurt. So, it was him she was seeing. Was it him she was texting this morning? The reason she had that smile upon her face? Did Adele have his beautiful number on her stupid phone? Did she tell him to leave the curtain open on purpose knowing, at some point, I would look out? No, it was unlike Adele. She wouldn't do this to me, or would she? I didn't know anymore. I should have been dragged by the hair out of the apartment and shot twice in the head for telling her about Alan. I should have kept it to myself. It made sense how Adele knew his name, was she already seeing him? Even though, somehow, I had no right for this anger. He wasn't my boyfriend; I didn't know the guy it was pathetic really, yet the betrayal that my friend would do this to me. I wanted to shut the curtain, to stop watching like some kind of pervert, but it was like I was leaving my body. Alan unclipped her bra and her breasts came free. I took in her small breasts and her dark nipples, her flat stomach and the belly ring. The butterfly tattoo on her outer thigh. My heart drummed in my ears. How did they meet? Why didn't Adele tell me? That was what hurt the most, that Adele didn't have the decency to tell me. Of course, she didn't owe me anything, but there was a code between women. Especially among friends. My chest rose and fell, heavy and painful.

Alan's blue eyes were like lasers burning me. My jaw dropped. I was slammed back into my body. Adele was oblivious, too engrossed in the sensuality to notice. I yanked the curtains, almost tearing them down, and shut them closed.

Chapter Two

It was like the room had been enveloped in ice. My chest heaved in and out. It hurt to breathe.

Shit! Shit! Shit!

Fuck! Fuck! Fuck!

He saw me.

So much for the guy who I thought didn't know I existed. He knew now. As the one who was watching him undressing my friend. I moved away from the curtain as if it would burn me. I paced in the bedroom, my heart racing. I stared at the wall, then turned and gaped through the curtain, only slightly so just my eye could fit. His bedroom light was off. Were they having sex in the dark? That was odd. Was it? Have I imagined the whole spectacle? No, it was too real to be imagined.

I moved away from the curtain and blinked. So, Adele was dating or sleeping with the guy she knew I liked and didn't tell me about it. Did Adele think I wouldn't find out? Well, she always took me for a fool, but I knew which side my bread was buttered. Then another thought wafted in. What if he told her I saw them?

Adele came home, I'm not sure at what time, but I was wide awake. I lay on the bed, still, as if she would hear me breathe. I heard her cough and move about in her bedroom before there was silence. I didn't sleep at all. Each time I shut my eyes, I saw Adele and Alan and his eyes struck me like a thunderbolt.

The next morning, I sat by the kitchen counter with my cereal. I made a bowl for Adele too, unlike her, where she never poured milk on mine, I poured milk on hers so by the time she'd be ready; it went all soft. I never did this before, but today was no ordinary day. It was the least she deserved. I was sipping my coffee when she came out, flipping her long blonde hair. I watched her closely, her face had that post-coital glow and my heart thundered. She muttered good morning, poured coffee in a blue mug, and sat across from me. Adele wrinkled her nose at the bowl but said nothing about the cereal drowned in milk.

'Did you have a good night?' I asked.

Her phone beeped and she jumped to it. Was it Alan telling her what a great night he had? Were the words *great sex*-typed somewhere on that phone? His image was forever tainted by the picture of them in bed together. My body tensed.

'What?' she asked after she replied to whoever it was.

Did she add him on Facebook too? Would she declare her relationship status to him in the future? My jealousy was alive and seething. I took a sip of coffee. The liquid-filled me with warmth like a hug.

'You seem distracted,' I said.

'I'm sorry, I'm preoccupied,' she said. 'I had a long night.'

I stood taking my backpack. That you did, I thought, that you did. If I had such a fox in my bed, sleep was the last thing I would do. I left from the back door. I was reluctant to use the front door, afraid I'd run into him. I never did, but now I didn't know if he'd make it a point that we'd run into each other. Why would someone leave the curtain open when they were about to have sex? Somehow, I couldn't shake the feeling that whole act, leaving the curtain open, him looking straight at me, was directed at me and I didn't know why. It freaked me out and I was alarmed. What could he do? Confront me? It would be embarrassing to stand there and talk about something so intimate when he didn't know me. But we had Adele floating between us, a connection, something we had in common.

During lunch, I was out in the yard eating a sandwich with a book I wasn't reading and replying to Tom's text. I didn't tell him about Adele, it was silly to mention it and he wouldn't understand; even though we were close, we weren't so close as to discuss our love troubles. He had been in a steady relationship for two years with Holly. My brother worked in IT, Holly in marketing. Greg walked past and stopped. I tried not to groan in frustration. Greg was a fellow student, studying English literature with Adele, and I suspected he had a crush on me. Greg was tall, around six feet two, with ginger hair like a carrot, that sort of thing.

'Hey, Phoebe,' he said.

'Hey,' I said.

'What are you reading?'

I showed him the book that I wasn't reading. *The Children of Men*.

'I never read it,' he said. 'Is it any good?'

'Yes, it's brilliant,' I lied.

He stared at me, lingering there.

'Yes?' I asked.

'Sorry, I just...'

'You just what?'

'I thought...'

'You thought what?'

He went red.

I rolled my eyes.

'Nothing...' he said. 'Anyway, see you around.'

Janice walked towards us, her backpack slung over one shoulder and holding a set of books and her phone. Greg glanced at her, took one last glance at me and stomped off.

Janice stopped in front of me, I had to lift my hand to shield the sun.

'Is he bothering you?' she asked.

'No, he just came over for a chat.'

She swung her foot from side to side. 'Is Adele okay?'

'Why shouldn't she be?' I asked.

'Oh, I don't know. She hardly hangs out with us anymore.'

'Really?' I asked, unable to mask my surprise.

'Yeah, it's been over a month now. We ask her to go out with us but since she's seeing a guy now it all makes sense.'

Adele had been seeing Alan for a month? When was she planning to tell me?

'Maybe it's the real thing,' I said.

Janice shrugged. 'Could be, she's not ready to share him yet.'

Such bullshit, I thought.

'Well, you know how she is when a guy is in the picture,' I said.

Adele was the person who, once there was a guy involved, hardly makes time for her friends. She disappears into this haze when it comes to guys. Janice and Hannah had been her friends long enough to know this. Adele met them when we started university. When things went sour with the guy she was dating, Adele turned to her friends again. It was selfish and she had lost friends because of this. Adele thought they were jealous of her because she was beautiful, but it wasn't the case.

'Have you met him?' Janice asked, pulling me back to reality.

'No,' I said.

'Hmm…' she said. 'So, if Greg asks you out, would you go out with him?'

It was an odd question coming from her. We weren't friends, more like acquaintances.

'No,' I admitted, looking in the direction Greg had gone.

'I think you should. He's cute.' She checked her watch and her eyes widened. 'Oh bugger, I have to go. I'm going to be late for class,' she said and walked off.

I didn't want to date anyone from the university. I didn't shit where I ate. I didn't trust students, especially the male ones. Not after the experience I'd had.

The curtains were wide open when I arrived at the apartment. I was sure they were closed before I left. I called out for Adele, but silence answered me back. She must have opened them before she left, but Adele hardly ever opened them. I didn't think she was aware we had curtains. I walked to the window and could see Alan's apartment clearly from where I stood. It didn't look like he was there.

Adele didn't show up and I stayed home and studied. I cooked her dinner but if she was meeting Alan, Adele would probably have dinner with him, if they did that sort of thing. I wondered what they did together. Were they the couple who went on long strolls holding hands, went to movies, had dinner in a nice restaurant? Or stayed in and focused on their carnal desires? While I had my dinner, I went through Adele's photos on Facebook and scrolled through her friend list. She had 3,000 friends to my modest 132. As if she knew all those people. Most of them were men, naturally. I tried to look for Alan, but I didn't know his second name. Names and faces went past and blended into one, but it didn't look like Adele had him on there. How they'd met I very much wanted to know, and I was being pathetic. I should move on. This wasn't healthy for me or our friendship.

Chapter Three

Adele showed her face less and less in the apartment during the evenings, and I knew she wasn't far away. I wondered if she knew that I knew. It didn't seem Alan had told her I saw them together, and if he did; she didn't tell me.

I have seen them again while peering out of the window. I had to stop doing it, but I couldn't help myself. There was the light of the TV, and a bottle of wine on the coffee table, along with two glasses. Adele was sitting on Alan's lap. I only made a gap between the curtains where my eyes would fit. I had to avoid fuck ups. I didn't want to be caught spying on them by him again.

In the mornings, I kept pouring milk in Adele's cereal and watched it go soft. It became an unspoken language between us.

Weeks went by and I became a gap in the curtain. I could burn a hole through them. It wasn't the seeing her with him that made me so angry, but her not telling me about it. I decided to stop being a coward and go out from the front door. I kept my head low, but I never ran into him. It was like he was this gorgeous vision that appeared at specific times in that apartment. Like an apparition or a dream.

In the evening, I ran myself a bath and lay there watching the steam swallowing the room. Adele was out again. At this rate, she'd fail all her finals if she didn't catch up. However, Adele had the rare talent of passing every exam without touching a book. Some people have all the luck. Having a bath was some sort of event for me. I had no sex life. No boyfriend. So, I had to make do with what I had. I creased my breast and pinched my nipple hard until it stood to attention. I closed my eyes and saw Alan standing in his bedroom, Adele topless, her back to him, her eyes closed and his cold icy stare on me. I opened my eyes and composed myself. Adele had to ruin my fantasy too.

I'd gone to the kitchen to make myself a cup of coffee when Adele came in. She was early, maybe Mr Handsome next door had things to do tonight or she was overstaying her welcome.

'Oh, you're back early,' I said and bit my bottom lip.

I shouldn't have said that. I didn't want to give her the impression I was monitoring her.

'Yes, I need to catch up on my studies, I'm so behind,' Adele said, placing her oversized handbag on the stool.

'Coffee?' I asked.

She shook her head. 'There's something I have to tell you.'

'Oh,' I said. 'I'll get dressed.'

From the sorry look upon her face, I could tell it was confession time. So, it was serious after all.

'No, it's important and you are dressed,' she pointed out.

'No, I'm in my bathrobe.'

'Phoebe, please.'

I walked past her carrying my mug. 'After I get dressed.'

I put on a black jumper and a pair of leggings, taking my time. Torturing her a little. Adele was sitting by the kitchen counter with a glass of wine and she had poured one for me.

'What do you want to talk to me about?' I asked, sitting across from her.

Adele took a sip of wine and pressed her lips together, more to wet them than to drink. I kept my hands clasped together on the counter as if I were in a job interview. She looked at me then glanced away, shaking her head.

'God, you make this more difficult than it already is,' she said in her sultry voice.

By sultry, I mean Adele always talked like this. Adele had this seductive voice, measured, like she'd had a vocal coach who taught her to talk in such a collected, low voice, but she just talked like this, like she just got out of bed.

'How so?'

'Stop it, Phoebe, drink some wine and relax, you're always so composed, so in control.'

'Is this what you want to talk to me about, my self-control?' I asked, lifting an eyebrow at her.

'I'm seeing Alan!'

It came out as a shout which took me aback because Adele didn't shout. Adele broke eye contact and took a large gulp of wine.

The silence was deafening. I reached for the glass of wine and drained it. Adele watched me curiously.

'Oh,' I said.

'That's all you have to say. God, Phoebe. It's hard for people to warm to you.'

Why was she talking to me as if I were the arsehole? I've done nothing wrong. If there was an arsehole among us, it was her.

'How long have you been seeing him?' I asked, ignoring her statement.

She fingered the rim of her glass. 'About a month or so.'

'A month and you're telling me now?' I asked.

'I wasn't sure that it could be serious,' she said.

'And it is… serious?'

She glanced at me. 'I'm not sure.'

'Where did you meet him?'

'At a club.'

'At a club?'

'Yes, where people dance and drink, have fun, try it sometime, it's quite extraordinary.'

'I don't think you have any right to be patronising,' I snapped. 'And you're telling me this because?'

'Because you like him, I mean... I watched you glue yourself to that window and I feel bad,' she said pouring more wine for herself, none for me.

But not enough to stop you from fucking him, I wanted to tell her. I poured more wine and took a gulp, pushing the words back.

'Well... it's not like I dated him or something, so it means nothing,' I said.

'But I feel guilty. I don't want to lose a friendship over this.'

As if she cared about our friendship when he was inside her.

'It's cool. I'm over it already. Want to watch an episode of *Friends* and order a pizza?' I suggested.

She blinked at me. 'I told you I have to study. I'm behind.'

Maybe she should spend less time with him. I wanted to tell her this but bit my tongue.

I met Tom in a café close to the university. I got there early, so I ordered a cup of instant black coffee and a cupcake while I waited. Fifteen minutes later, Tom walked in dressed in a black suit and with his laptop case with the red strap hanging on his shoulder. This image of him always made me smile with the black case and the red strap. My brother and I had similar looks, he had short black hair and angular features, the slight difference, his eyes were blue, mine were brown. We hugged and he placed his case on the floor and sat across from me.

'You look smart,' I said.

'Yeah... I had a day full of meetings. How are things with you? How is your studying going?'

'Oh good,' I said.

He flagged the passing waitress and ordered a vanilla latte.

'Vanilla latte, that's so girly,' I teased.

'Shut up, you know I like vanilla.'

'How's Mum and Dad?'

'They're good. When are you coming over for lunch?'

'I don't know, I have exams soon.'

'Oh, come on, can't you take a break for two hours and join us for a Sunday roast?'

'I'll see what I can do.'

The waitress placed Tom's latte in front of him and I watched him tear a packet of sugar and stir it in his drink.

'I'm thinking of proposing,' he said.

A feeling of joy rushed through me; my brother was getting engaged.

'Oh my God, that's lovely, when are you thinking of doing it?'

'I'm thinking of booking a surprise holiday. Holly always wanted to go to Rome.'

'Rome, that's so romantic…' I gushed, bursting with happiness for him. 'This is so exciting, have you told Mum and Dad? They'll be over the moon!'

'No, not yet,' he said and glanced at me quickly. 'You're the first person I've told.'

'Don't worry, I won't tell them. You know I can keep a secret.'

I stood and went to hug him. Tom didn't do well with hugs and after a few seconds he pulled away, and I went back to my seat.

'I'm nervous,' he said.

'I think it's natural to feel that way.'

'What if she says no?'

'Holly saying no? She would say yes in a heartbeat, she adores you.'

'Would she?'

'Of course, she would,' I assured him. 'It will be fine, you'll see, it will be more than fine, it will be wonderful. When are you going?'

'I don't know yet… soon though.'

We sipped our coffee in silence. 'So how is Adele? Still breaking hearts?' Tom asked.

Tom wasn't Adele's biggest fan. He didn't like the Barbie-doll image. I lowered my eyes and wondered if Adele would burst through the door one day, all glowing with a diamond ring on her finger.

'What's wrong? What has she done now?' Tom asked, slamming me back to the present.

'What makes you think she's done something?'

He pulled a funny face. 'This is Adele we're talking about.'

'It's silly,' I said.

'I don't care, you're my sister, I'm interested.'

I took a sharp inhale of breath. After I finished telling him what had happened, Tom shook his head in disbelief.

'We both know Adele has a hard time keeping her legs closed, but I honestly don't see how you two lasted as friends, she's using you.'

'Using me?'

'Yeah, using you, to be her housekeeper and take your guys too.'

'Alan isn't my guy.'

'Still, it's not nice. It says a lot about her and about her character, to be honest. What are you going to do about it?' he asked.

The questions threw me off guard. What am I going to do about it? What could I do? Beat her up, move out and move back with my parents. I could do that, but it was ridiculous to do that over something so petty.

Chapter Four

'Excuse me,' I said.

'You and I are going out for dinner,' Adele announced.

It was unusual for her to suggest dinner in a restaurant with tables, chairs and waiters. Usually, her taking me out for dinner comprised a place where we took our food and had no waiters.

'I have to study,' I said.

She rolled her eyes. 'So do I. You can take a break. We both can.'

'So, you made a reservation?' I asked incredulously.

'Yes, at eight so put on something nice. Dinner is on me.'

'Why didn't you tell me about this dinner?'

Another eye roll. 'I wanted to surprise you.'

I moved the curtain about an inch. His apartment lights were on. For a horrifying second, I thought this dinner was an ambush to introduce me to him. I didn't want to meet Alan. I knew he was there. I had this projected image of him and if I met him in person, it would be ruined but I had to meet him at some point or another. I got dressed in red velvet bodycon dress and applied makeup and wore high heels, something I haven't done in a long time; dress up and go out on the town.

'You look amazing. Stunning,' Adele said.

Adele kept touching her ear and twirling her finger into her hair. In the taxi, she didn't stop babbling. It went on and on, first about classes, then about her mum, then about this dress she bought and about forgetting to book an appointment for her hair.

'Should I paint my nails red?' she asked.

'I've read it drives men crazy,' I said.

'Do you have red nail varnish? I don't think I do.'

'You know I don't wear nail polish,' I said.

She sighed dramatically. 'Oh, Phoebe, make more effort.'

I pulled a face. 'Because I don't wear nail varnish it doesn't mean I don't make an effort,' I protested.

'That is not what I meant… when was the last time you dated someone?' she asked.

'My priorities, for now, are to get on with my studies, not boys.' I said.

Adele rolled her eyes.

The restaurant had marble floors, tables dressed in white cloths with flowers and candles, and a pianist playing in the background. It screamed expensive and high class. I opened the menu. There was no way Adele could afford this extravagance. She worked part-time as a waitress on weekends. I worked from home doing bookkeeping for a small accountancy firm. I couldn't afford this either. Maybe she'd got the money from her parents, but I didn't want her to spend that much on me. She ordered a bottle of wine. The restaurant screamed *I'm trying too hard*. Had Alan brought her to this place? Was that how she knew about it? Adele didn't do fine dining restaurants; she was more a kebab sort of girl after a night out of drinking and partying.

Was this her way to treat me to something for what she did? It was offensive; she had the gorgeous bloke and I'd be the one who got an expensive meal. Adele should have let us get on with our lives. This grand gesture was making it worse as if I was an object to be pitied. The starter arrived which we shared between us, a basil parmesan cheesecake with tomato jam. It was, of course, delicious.

'How did you get the money to pay for all of this?' I asked.

The waiter came over and poured white wine into our empty glasses.

'I saved up,' Adele said, not making eye contact.

She was lying. Each time Adele told a lie, she had a habit of not looking the person in the eye.

'Is he paying for this?' I asked.

Her eyes levelled with mine. I was expecting him to walk in any minute. I dropped my napkin on the table and Adele's eyes widened with panic.

'Please, don't make a scene. I'm doing something nice here.'

'Yeah, by having him pay for this, thank you very much. If you wanted to do something nice, you could have ordered Indian or a pizza.'

She ran her hand through her hair. 'I feel you're not over it.'

'I am. We will not fight over some hot guy,' I sighed.

But most of our disagreements were about guys and Adele's inability to keep her legs closed.

'But this is not the first time it's happened,' Adele pointed out.

'Well, you're a beautiful girl and bubbly. Men like that.'

'And you're gorgeous too, but you're hard to connect with.' she said.

'Oh, am I? And who are you to make such remarks, you and I connected, didn't we?'

'You know you are and we have been friends for a long time but people who don't know you, they can get… intimidated.'

How dare she sit there and say those things to me when she didn't have the decency to pay for this dinner from her own pocket? I didn't want her or his charity.

'I want you to meet him,' Adele blurted out.

So, this what it was alluding to, all this talk about being hard to connect with, not making enough effort, blah, blah, blah.

'So, you're a couple now?'

'I told you it could get serious and you're my best friend,' Adele said. 'I really like him. He's amazing.'

Of course, she liked him and I was sure he was amazing.

'I thought I'd tell you first so you won't be... challenging.'

Tom's words came to me about how our friendship had lasted so long. Each time I was interested in a guy, she'd stepped in and stolen him away. There was a guy I'd liked; his name was Adam. I went on a few dates with him, then I caught him and Adele having coffee, looking very much *into* each other. I confronted her and she burst into tears. She'd continued to see him for three months until she'd became interested in someone else. I forgave her because I didn't want to lose a friendship. Was Adele afraid of losing a friendship? The thing was, Adele had other friends, she had Janice and Hannah while me, I had nobody. I had no other friends apart from Adele. Might as well see what this guy was all about. If he was worth all the drama.

'Fine. I'll meet him,' I said.

Adele's large blue eyes sparkled. 'You will?'

'Sure.'

'This makes me so happy.'

But she didn't give a damn about my happiness.

The taxi dropped us in front of the apartment. As we stepped out, Adele told me she was going over to Alan's. My eyes went to his flat, Alan was by the window watching us. Adele blew him a kiss. He responded with a smile.

'I'd better go in.' I said.

Adele wrapped her arms around me, and I inhaled her strawberry scented shampoo. My eyes went to his window and Alan was still there staring at us.

Chapter Five

'You are what?' Tom said exasperated when he called.

'She wants me to meet him.'

'And you said yes?'

'What can I do? I live with her, I can't say no.'

'Oh, Phoebe, next thing you know she'll be asking you to hold their clothes while they have sex.'

I heard voices behind the front door, Adele laughing at something Alan might have said.

'I have to go. I'll call you later,' I told him and hung up.

I puffed my face as butterflies flew in my stomach. I hated orchestrated meetings. All this pretending. I felt like I was being held captive, tied down to a chair and taking blow after blow, each one more painful than the last. I would have avoided this all together if I could, but I was trapped. I didn't know what to do.

When Alan stood in the flesh in front of me, I couldn't get over how gorgeous he truly was; in a way, my eyes bled. Too beautiful for words. It hurt to look at him. His blue eyes had a hint of grey in them. His eyelashes were so long it looked like he had makeup on. His face was oval with a set of sharp and high cheekbones. A straight nose. He was nearly six feet tall, towering over both of us, and the quiff perfected with hairspray made him taller. There was no way a guy like that would notice someone like me. He was better suited to Adele. He, however, wasn't afraid of making eye contact as if he wanted to tell me something. Meanwhile, I had to avoid the elephant in the room and stop myself from staring. He was dazzling. Stunning like a work of art, and he smelled like a five-star hotel. They bought me cupcakes, blue frosted ones, my favourite and I couldn't have been more insulted. Adele got to have that snack in her arms while I'd get to have the expensive meal and the cupcakes. It was depressing. Adele was babbling. As usual, they were having dinner. Would I like to join? I didn't want to sit across from this beautiful couple and play with my food and endure it. I played the "I have to study card" which made Adele back off. Alan gave me the impression that he was rather unfriendly, cold even. He barely said two words apart from the awkward hello and nice to meet you. We wouldn't make a good match. You couldn't have two cold people together. Someone had to provide the warmth, and Adele was perfect for that. They grew larger in front of me while I got smaller and smaller. As they moved away, I lingered by the door. Alan placed a hand around the small of Adele's back and cast an icy but seductive glance at me.

Once inside, I opened the box of cupcakes. They looked pretty and innocent. I took one then another and before I knew it, I'd eaten them all. Look at you the voice in my head roared, you ate all the cupcakes, you disgusting pig and you think a guy like that would take a second look at you? Dream on, hog.

Once the introductions had been made, it still didn't help the stiffness around Adele and me. She didn't give me full-on details of what he was like in bed, as she'd done with the other men she dated. Maybe she cared after all, and honestly, I didn't want to know. I was sure he was lovely and gave her plenty of earth-shattering orgasms. I knew they were there, that he was giving them to her, but I didn't have to hear about them. But Adele would slip here and there sometimes 'Oh, Alan hates these…' or 'Oh, yes, I went to that place with Alan.,' she would say then trail off as she remembered his name was banned from being mentioned around my presence as if it would cause me some kind of allergic reaction, which wasn't the case. I suspected Adele was being careful how to talk around me.

'I want you and Alan to be friends,' she told me one day in the cafeteria during lunch. Before Janice and Hannah came to join us. I took a large bite of sandwich and chewed slowly, then took another bite, filling my mouth like a hamster to buy me time. Adele's mouth twisted in disgust; she found me repulsive. It was how she said it that bugged me, it's the *I want* that irritated me. She demanded this of me, to make an effort, a request plain and simple. Not caring about my needs, which were simply to be left alone. If she'd said something between the lines like, *do you think you and Alan can be friends?* It would have sounded a lot better. She wouldn't stop rubbing it in, sticking the knife in deep and hard. Adele had wanted to introduce me to him, which I'd accepted. Now she wants us to be friends? Was Adele forcing me to like him, and him to like me as well? A picture was painted in her head and Adele wanted it to happen in real life. I had seen them again from my bedroom window. He had the window open and I wanted to yell at him from across the road, *close the fucking curtains.* Adele had her legs around him, leaning her against the wall. His lips were on her neck, her head tilted back, her hands in his hair. Adele had said it could be serious but from what I was seeing, it looked purely sexual to me but they were in the early stages in their relationship and a new coupling equals lots of sex. I wondered though what his true intentions were? Apart from the fact he was gorgeous, who was he? What did Adele know about him?

We sat across from each other, me, Adele and Alan. I was draining glasses of wine and he scowled at me, clearly not impressed, but I didn't care what he thought of me, or about leaving the right impression. He must have thought not only did I like to watch people have sex, but I was a pervert with a drinking problem. Those blue-grey eyes looked as if they could read me and I couldn't help but feel exposed so I drank to feel more confident, more secure. Did Adele tell him I had a crush on him? Was that why he was eyeing me in such a way?

'Finance,' he said incredulously.

Our handsome Alan had a glamorous job, a music producer. He was also a technical musician, Adele said as if he could not speak for himself, but she didn't elaborate how deep his technicality went because Adele didn't know. He was a classically trained pianist. Adele wasn't interested if he was the next Tchaikovsky or played like Bach. What she cared about was that he was good with his fingers. This guy sounded too good to be true.

'Yes,' I said.

'You sure look it,' he said.

He, also, could make me feel like I was down there right at the bottom, and he was above me. Did he think he sounded cool by making such a remark? It made him sound like a pompous arse. Adele burst out laughing. My eyes passed to her then landed on him.

'She does, doesn't she?' Adele laughed. 'We're only joking.'

I was the zoo animal held in captivity unable to enjoy the freedom and instead, I'd be mocked and displayed for people to see. I took more gulps of wine and again he scowled at me. What was his problem anyway? He'd already downed four pints of beer since we had been there, so he wasn't the right candidate to pass any judgement. Chill out music filled the chic lounge bar we were in. The people there were groomed, immaculate looking, sipping on their cocktails. Adele took a sip hers which was green and looked like slime. She stood and slid next to me and threw her arms lovingly around my shoulder.

'I'm so glad we're doing this. We're going to have so much fun,' she cooed.

What did she mean by that? What did Adele have in mind? We were going to hang out, the three of us, him, me and her one big happy family. I didn't think so.

'This makes me so happy,' she went on, kissing me on the cheek, which left a pink splotch of lipstick imprinted there. Her breath smelt of mint and vodka from the cocktail.

'She cares so much,' Adele said.

Alan watched us amused and took a sip from his pint.

'Unlike some.' I blurted.

I couldn't help myself. Adele didn't notice the jab, but Alan cast a sharp glance at me. Who was this guy?

Thanks to Google, you can do a quick search to find information about someone. But when I typed Alan Wiley

(Adele had told me his surname) all I got was the football referee. Alan Wiley is a common name. I tapped my fingers on my laptop, thinking about what to type to narrow the search down. I typed music producer behind his name. *Nothing.* I typed Alan Wiley, not the football referee, you'll never know, right? *Nothing.* Alan Wiley classically trained pianist. Not a damn thing. If he was a music producer, even if he wasn't well known, wouldn't there be something about him? Or the artists he worked with? It seemed strange there was nothing about this bloke; it was as if he was a ghost. No Facebook page, no Twitter account, no Instagram either. He was invisible. I went to Adele's Facebook and stalked her friends list again, but nothing. No Alan Wiley. *Weird.* I didn't think Adele dated anyone who didn't have at least one social media account. It's not uncommon for people not to be on Facebook or Twitter. I hardly ever used mine. But Adele was all about Facebook. All the time, she plastered the phone in my face, snapping photos. I scrolled into her feed hoping for a photo of her with Alan to pop up. Dating a guy who looked like that, she had to share him with the world. *Look at my prize, my boyfriend is better, hotter than yours,* her feed would scream. Not a trace of him. What I did notice though, was her relationship status, it had been switched from *single* to *complicated*. What was so complicated about their relationship? It seemed straightforward to me

Chapter Six

Alan wasn't the only exotic addition to our lives. His friend, Dylan joined this bubble Adele was creating. Dylan, just like Alan, was extremely good looking. He had a sandy complexion, dark brown eyes and short dark hair with blonde highlights. Adele must have put Alan up to this, trying to set me up with his friend. I played along just to amuse myself. I wondered if, in time, Adele would switch from Alan to Dylan and destroy a perfectly healthy relationship between the boys. Adele had done it before and couldn't understand what she could have done wrong.

'I know what you're going to do all day,' Dylan was telling me.

We were in a pub, bottles of beer were on the table along with bowls of peanuts. The loud chatter from the TV boomed around us.

'You'll get the guys to photocopy your arse,' he said.

I threw my head back and laughed. Adele and Alan laughed too.

'So, no one in your family works in finance?' Dylan asked.

'No, my mum was a secretary and my father is a vet, and my brother works in IT,' I said.

'Was?' Alan asked.

'What? I asked.

'You said your mum *was*,' he remarked.

How very observant.

'She stopped working when she got pregnant with my brother,' I said.

'You didn't consider taking after your father?' Dylan asked.

I hate when the spotlight shines on me. I took a sip of beer. 'No, not for me.'

'Not an animal lover?' Alan asked.

Why so interested?

'I love animals, but I couldn't do the things my father does,' I replied.

Alan nodded as if he understood, and his eyes shifted back to the football game on the TV.

'What about you, Adele, with your English literature, are you hoping to become the next Margaret Atwood?' Dylan asked.

'I wish,' she said.

'What you're going to do with that degree?' Alan asked.

Adele glanced at her shoes, frowning. 'I don't know… teach, maybe.'

I couldn't see Adele as a teacher. I pictured her doing something more glamorous like marketing, PR, or in fashion even.

'As if,' Alan laughed.

She playfully slapped his arm. 'You know what you should do.'

'What?' Alan asked.

'Have a party at your place.'

Alan glared at Adele as if this was the stupidest thing he had ever heard. 'And why would I do that?'

'I think it would be nice,' she said.

'For what reason would I throw a party, anyway?' His eyes went back to the screen.

'Do you need a reason to throw a party?' she said, taking out her phone. 'We should take a picture of the four of us.'

We posed for a photo and Adele squeaked in delight.

'Don't put it up on Facebook,' Alan warned.

And why the hell not? I thought. What he had to hide?

When we arrived home, Adele placed her bag on the dresser by the door and went to the kitchen. I had to tell her about Alan not being anywhere online. I was sure there was a logical explanation for this and I would expose myself for prying, but despite everything, she was my friend. I followed her into the kitchen. Adele opened the fridge and poured herself a glass of Coke.

'Besides the fact Alan is unbelievably gorgeous, what do you know about him?' I asked.

She glared at me. 'Everything that I need to know.'

'Which is?'

'That's hardly any of your business,' Adele hissed, and turning away from me, she went to the living room and flumped down on the sofa.

'I'm your friend, it's my job to worry and ask you those things… I looked him up.'

Her eyes went wide. 'You did *what*?'

'There is nothing on him. Not a damn thing. It doesn't strike you as odd? It's like this guy doesn't even exist!'

Her eyes were frantic now. 'I see. So, you're still bitter about me dating your crush and you went to look him up to make up a story about him?'

'If he's a music producer, as he claims to be, how come there is no information about him anywhere? What about the artists he's worked with? Shouldn't he be credited somewhere? And if he were a pianist, wouldn't there be anything about it?'

'I don't know. Why don't you ask him since you are so interested? I'm only interested in what he does for me, you know… sex-wise.'

'So, you're not interested in Alan at all, you're just with him for his looks and the fact that he's great in bed, is that what you're trying to tell me?'

'That's exactly what I'm telling you; you're just jealous because I'm getting some while you aren't!' she snarled and stomped off to her bedroom, slamming the door shut to make a statement.

And she said I was the cold one?

That night I twisted and turned on the bed, unable to get any sleep. Adele seemed so unconcerned about the whole thing. I left my bedroom and the light was on under Adele's bedroom door. I pressed my ear to the door and faint cries and sighs came from behind it. I moved away from the door as it was on fire. She wasn't alone. Alan was with her. What was this a hotel? Unable to contain my fury, I stomped to the bathroom, opened the medicine cabinet, and found the bottle of sleeping pills. I didn't take them regularly, not wanting to depend on them, but that night, I needed them. My mum had taken me to a doctor because I had trouble sleeping because of the stress and anxiety while I was doing my exams. I popped a pill in my mouth and dry swallowed it. I left the bathroom and walked back to my room, glancing at the bedroom as if a monster would burst out of it and attack me. From behind the door came a bang, which made me jump. What were they doing there? I hurried to my bedroom and lay back on the bed, lifting the sheets to my chin. Adele was playing a game with me. She knew I liked this guy and now bringing him here for sex? Adele was doing it deliberately to hurt me.

Why, though? Why was she doing this? Do friends do this? What have I done to cause her this level of contempt?

Chapter Seven

The next morning, I showered, dressed and applied my makeup. I banged on her bedroom door.

'Would you like me to bring you two a cup of tea?' I said in a friendly voice.

'We're fine!' Adele said from behind the door.

I was sipping on my mug of coffee when the bedroom door opened and Alan was the first who came out. I could hear Adele move about as he shut the door.

'Good morning,' he said.

'Morning,' I mumbled.

He approached the counter. Did Adele tell him about what I told her? It was obvious her loyalty lay with him, not with me, her friend she'd known all her life. I stared up at him. Who was this man? Where did he come from? What did he want? Alan reached for an apple from the fruit basket. The clock went off and I jumped.

'See you later, Phoebe.' he said and winked.

If Adele was interested in what he could do for her sexually, I was interested in him as a person. Behind those crazy good looks, what sort of man lay under there?

When I arrived home that afternoon, Adele wasn't in yet and I didn't have to take a guess where she was or with who. The apartment was in complete disarray and Tom was coming over for dinner. I sighed and gathered Adele's clothes from all over the apartment. I went into her room and placed the clothes on her unmade bed. The room smelt of sex and cigarettes. Shaking my head, I opened the window, turned and took in the mess. Dirty underwear on the floor, bras hanging on the bedposts. Books scattered on the bedside table. Books she would never read. Her desk was in a different kind of state; pens and pencils were scattered there along with her notes, and her iPad lay underneath the mess. I turned facing the bedside table and a hardback caught my eye. The cover had black and white squares like tiles, *Lost and Found* was smeared in red like blood, Robert Freeman was the author. I creased my eyebrows; it wasn't a book I would find on Adele's bedside table. I turned it over. It was a crime fiction novel.

Cody had gone missing. He only took the money with him, nothing else. A search had been conducted, but Cody was never found. Now, his sister, Jenny has to find out what happened to her younger brother. She needs closure. Jenny investigates and finds out her brother was seeing a woman in secret. Jenny gets in touch with her, hoping the woman knows what happened to Cody.

Then, Jenny receives a letter with two words scribbled on it: Lost and Found.

I sit on the bed flipping through the pages, intrigued by the whole plot. There was no information about the author and an unknown publisher published the book. Adele didn't read crime. She usually read chick lit and classic novels. Who gave her this? Alan? I returned the book to where it had been and left Adele's bedroom, but I spent the afternoon thinking about that book.

Tom made it a point to come over when Adele wasn't around. I never understood why. I knew he wasn't her biggest fan, but I found this too extreme on his part. I cooked lasagne and he supplied the wine.

'So, you're telling me...' he said between mouthfuls, 'she wants you to hang out with them?'

'Yes.'

'I don't know what you're doing, to be honest, tell her to sod off.'

'The strangest thing is... I looked him up and...' I trailed off.

Tom raised an eyebrow. 'And?'

'I looked him up and there is nothing about him, and when I told Adele she accused me of being jealous.'

'Of course, she would say that.'

'Anyway, enough about me. How is Holly?'

'She's good... are you coming this Sunday, to our parents?'

'I'll try.'

'Better be with us than with Adele and her new man, don't you think?'

'That's for sure.'

He placed his fork down and reached for my hand. 'Phoebe, I want you to be careful.'

This gesture alarmed me. 'I'm always careful.'

'I know, but I can't help but feel that something strange is going on here. Adele insisting on you joining her with this Alan guy. You say there is nothing about him online. Her introducing you to his friend, it all seems… odd.'

'I'm sure there is a reasonable explanation.' I said.

'For what?'

'For everything.'

'Yeah, I hope so.' he said, tucking back into his meal.

'Come with us to a club,' Adele ordered.

'What club? Where?' I asked.

'Just get dressed and be ready in an hour, Alan and Dylan will meet us outside the apartment.'

'But—'

'It will be fun, you'll see.' Adele assured me.

The annoyance sparked in my blood as I got dressed in a black turtleneck and black jeans, my trademark look.

Adele went to a lot of trouble, her face a mask with makeup, dressed in a gold bodycon dress and heels. Alan and Dylan were waiting for us outside as Adele had instructed, smoking cigarettes. Dylan glanced at me and smiled, and I returned the gesture. He was another odd one. There was no trace of him online either, no social media accounts, nothing. It was as if these blokes dropped from another planet straight into our lives. In the taxi, Dylan and I sat next to each other with our knees kissing, while Adele and Alan sat across from us. Alan's hand was placed on her knee marking her as if she were his property while Adele was singing along to the lyrics of a song playing on the radio. Dylan was typing on his phone. The taxi stopped in front of a tatty building with faded blue paint. There was no sign with the name of the place, it looked run down and I thought it was shut. Alan and Dylan were the first to get out. Adele didn't notice we had arrived since she was engrossed in her phone. Alan held the door open like a gentleman. Ants crawled on my back and I shivered as something in the air felt sinister. Dylan lit a cigarette after princess Adele was out of the car. Dylan opened the door and we went in. The pub was gloomy. A fat bearded man sat by the bar clutching a pint. Behind the bar, a sad-looking man stood with his arms folded, dressed in a white tank top. There were four tables and at one of them, sat a man and woman playing cards. What was this place? What were we doing here? This didn't look like a club to me, just a dodgy little bar.

I was about to turn to leave when Adele grabbed my hand with a kind of strength I didn't know she possessed. Her red polished nails dug into my skin and I winced slightly.

'Don't you even think about it!' she hissed.

What was it with her? What was her problem? Why she was being like this? Adele pushed me forward, almost knocking me into Alan and he glared back at me, while I felt like a sacrificial lamb. Dylan walked to the back and pushed open a red door I hadn't noticed before. Where were they taking me? What was this? The door led to a long corridor with red lights. One of them was flickering. Adele's heels echoed. Or was it the slamming of my heart? We went down the three steps and Dylan pushed another door to yet another corridor. We marched along, our footsteps echoing through the walls. Water dripped from one of the pipes, and the overpowering smell of piss filled my nostrils. I wanted to go home to bed. Alan stopped walking, which led to me almost crashing into him, again. He held out his hand and I stupidly stood there trying to understand what this gesture meant. Adele handed him her phone.

'You too,' he said to me.

'You want me to give you my phone?' I asked incredulously.

'Yes,' he said without giving me an explanation of why he wanted to part me from my phone.

'Why?'

A hand slid into the pocket of my coat, taking my phone. It was Adele and she handed it to Alan. I stared at her with my mouth gaping open like a fish. The influence he had on her, how she jumped to each of his requests. So eager to please and keep him happy. Like a little puppet. The anger coiled into me like lava. Who did she think she was anyway, giving him my phone without an explanation?

'Bitch.' I said, moving away from her.

Dylan opened another door and house music swallowed me. There were two staircases with red carpet, and a chandelier jingling on the ceiling, its lights glittering like diamonds. We descended the stairs and sweat broke on my back. My turtleneck itched my skin. There were two cages by the bar. On top of the bar was a Japanese woman dressed in a PVC skirt and a matching bra. Her long black hair cascaded to her back. Lying face down on the bar was a fat, shirtless man. My jaw dropped. I wasn't a prude, but I have never seen anything like this before. Dylan looked up at the woman. She smiled and winked at him.

'First round is on me,' Dylan said.

Had Alan taken our phones away so we wouldn't take any pictures of this secret night club hidden underground? Adele lingered by Alan. I scanned the dance floor where people were dancing in a suggestive, sexual sort of way. Was this their idea of a joke? Alan and Dylan moved along to the side of the club, past the sequined red curtain. There were black doors that were closed; God knew what was going on behind them. They walked to the room at the far end with plush purple sofas and women dancing in gold bikinis. Adele's face was passive. Had she been here before? The guys settled down on the sofa. Adele, still with the same expression on her face, sat down too. A blonde dancer came over and set her sights on Dylan and Alan.

'Well, well, aren't we cute?' she said.

She performed a lap dance on Alan, rubbing her body against his crotch. He laughed, turning red, while the woman continued with her fake theatrical show to arouse the men. She took off her bikini top, exposing large breasts. I measured her fake breasts to mine. Big, perky. Perfect. Whereas mine were not full and not so round and not perfect.

'Your girlfriend is very beautiful,' she said to Alan.

I thought she was referring to Adele, but the woman was looking at me. Alan glanced at me but didn't correct the dancer which was strange. Adele had her hands clutched into fists as if at any moment, she was going to lurch at the dancer. The dancer turned to Dylan, and Alan sipped his beer and placed his hand on Adele's knee. She jumped as if she'd been asleep and was awakened by his touch. Adele looked at him, then up at the dancer who was rubbing her crotch against Dylan. Adele stood and I glanced up. Her face was still the same, passive, not showing anything but she stomped out of the room.

Chapter Eight

I frantically searched for her among the unfamiliar faces. I couldn't spot her, as if she'd vanished in thin air. Great, Alan had both of our phones and I had no means of contacting her. I went back to the room, but Dylan and Alan were gone. Brilliant. The bathroom, I thought. Adele might be in there. One problem, I didn't know where it was and there were no signs that showed where I could locate it. I went back to where I'd come from, through the corridors and opened doors. In the first room, there was a man on all fours and a woman in leather. She screamed at me, but the music muffled her shouting. The other was a dark, empty room. Another had two women getting dressed. The next door led to the bathroom. The room was foggy with smoke. A black woman was sitting on a chair by a plastic table. On it were tampons, sanitary towels, a body spray, hairbrushes, and condoms, along with a plate with small change. A woman stood by the mirror, powdering her face. Both women looked at me and returned to their conversations. They weren't speaking in English. I waited with my arms crossed. Each time a cubical door opened, I hoped it was Adele but it never was. The woman powdering her face wiggled away.

'Where is the exit?' I asked the black woman.

'No exit,' the woman said.

'What do you mean there is no exit?'

'Exit no. At four am.'

Did I hear that right? Was I locked in this place until four am? That meant I was locked in! How did Adele leave then? Okay, let's regroup, I thought. If we were locked in, that meant Adele was still on the premises. I left the bathroom and looked for her among the faces on the dance floor. The lights glowed from red to purple to green, and the music was so loud my ears were ringing. I went to the bar and ordered a shot of vodka. I needed it to get me through the night. Where were Alan and Dylan? I checked my watch; 2:00 am. I shook my head in dismay. What was I going to do in this club for the next two hours? Adele wasn't anywhere to be seen. *Love to Love You* was pumping from the speakers. I looked at the gliding crowds and Alan walked through the dance floor with ease and lit a cigarette. Was this his idea? It had to be. Adele wouldn't come to a place like this, although, I felt I didn't know her at all.

'Give me my phone now,' I said.

He gazed down at me puffing on his cigarette.

'Now!'

He shoved his hand in his inner jacket pocket, producing my phone. As I was about to take it, he grabbed me by the waist and spun me around, making me face the dance floor. I tried to wriggle free from his grasp, but his grip was too strong. I glanced around. Two men were making out in the corner. A woman had her leg up against a man getting it on.

'You like to watch, don't you?'

His breath was hot in my ear.

'What?'

'Don't…' he said. 'You know I saw you.'

'I wasn't…'

He turned me around to face him. I groaned, feeling like a rag doll in his arms.

'Are you trying to deny it?' he asked.

'You shouldn't leave the curtains wide open if you don't like people to look in. I know you did it on purpose.'

'Now why would I do that?'

'I have no idea. Why didn't you tell her?'

'Tell her what?'

My cheeks grew red. 'That I…'

'Why would I?' he asked.

I spotted Dylan by the far corner talking to another bloke. My breath caught in my throat. The music changed and the beat of a song was so heavy it vibrated into my brain. He pulled away and glanced up at something. My eyes followed what he was looking at, Adele was on top of a box, dancing. I blinked rapidly to let my eyes adjust. What a weird, unusual night this had been. A glass appeared before me. I looked down at it, then up at who was holding it and took it from Alan's hand. He raised his eyebrow at me and continued to drink, turning his full attention to Adele. He waved at her and she swung her hips at him in return. He stood between us, in our way, between our friendship or what was left of it. I wasn't sure if he was set on a path to destroy what we had left or bring us closer. The music was doing my head in. Adele looked at us; her eyes set on her man or fuck buddy or whatever he was.

The sun was so bright, I thought I was going to melt. I was lying face down on something, a sofa. I groaned as my head thumped and throbbed. There were traces of my saliva on the arm of the sofa and my mouth was dry and tasted like shit. I placed my hand on my forehead as I attempted to get up, and a jolt of pain in my muscles made me lay back on my stomach. I lay there for a while listening to the silence. It took a while to sink in that I wasn't on our sofa, that this wasn't our flat. I sat up straight, ignoring the ache in my body, and scanned the apartment in horror. How did I get here? Whose apartment was this?

The living room was large and brightly lit. There was a large rug with a tribal design on top of the parquet floors.

There was a wide bookshelf and all the furniture was made of pine. I rubbed the sofa's arm as if it would make the circle of my saliva go away. I looked up at the naïve art painting hanging on the wall and blinked at the fine grand piano. The entire apartment was stylish and neat. So neat, I was afraid to touch anything. A contrast to our Ikea furnished flat. I looked over my shoulder and I could see our apartment right across the road. I was in Alan's apartment. I surveyed myself as a rush of panic rolled through me, I was fully dressed and it didn't seem I'd done something I would regret later. Had I? I stood, steadying myself on the sofa; I placed my hand on my throbbing temples. The hangover swept through me. I haven't felt like this in ages. I wasn't that person, I didn't handle hangovers well. Unlike Adele, she handled them like a pro. A door opened from the far corner of the flat and Adele appeared, looking fresh-faced in jeans and T-shirt while I was still in clothes that smelt of cigarettes.

'Morning,' she giggled, 'that was an awesome night.'

'If your definition of awesome is feeling like this the next day,' I said.

The curtains in our apartment were open. I was sure they were closed the night before. I remember doing it. I pointed my finger at our flat. Adele came over and wrapped her arms around my waist.

'I'm sorry, I can be such a bitch sometimes. I can't help it. You know I don't mean it, right?'

I blinked at her. This was the Adele I knew, not the one who was around Alan.

'I love you,' she said, looking deeply into my eyes.

Adele kissed me on the cheek, her fingers playing with the hem of my turtleneck. I stood still, holding my foul breath. What was she trying to do?

'You have such a beautiful body. It's a shame you hide in these,' she said, lifting the top, exposing my stomach.

'Adele, what are—'

'Shhh,' she said. 'You talk too much. Relax, go with the flow.'

A motorcycle rumbled by and there was a smell of cherry blossom in the apartment. Where was Alan? I couldn't get over how clean this place was. How he put up with someone as disorganised and messy as Adele was beyond me. Adele had removed my top and was running her hand over my shoulder. I stood in this unfamiliar apartment in my jeans and bra. Adele's hands glided down to my chest and cupped my breasts. What was this? I searched her face. She was beautiful, but I never thought of her that way. I wasn't attracted to her or women. Adele had been with women, she wasn't shy in expressing her escapades. Adele was more sexually open and I envied the sexual freedom she possessed. Adele liked to experiment.

Her motto was if you want to try something, do it at least once. However, ever since she started seeing— correction—sleeping with Alan, her sexuality has become more vibrant, more alive, as if he unleashed something else within her.

'We can be together, you know,' she whispered, running her hand through my hair.

'Who?'

'Us.'

'Us?'

'You, me, and Alan.'

'*What?*'

'I'm sure he wouldn't mind. I mean, you want him… don't you? I see the way you look at him. How your eyes linger on him with such longing. It's not my fault we have the same taste in guys,' she said, her lips brushing against mine as she ran a finger over the curve of my breasts.

My body didn't react to her touch and her hands were icy cold.

'You can experience and enjoy him like I am,' she whispered. 'Only I'll be there.'

I shut my eyes and took a deep breath, dreaming of a glass of water.

'That dancer is right, you are beautiful,' Adele went on.

She kissed my neck and I opened my eyes. This was going too far. I wasn't sure if I liked the new direction our friendship was taking. How could we remain the same if it went further? But we hadn't been the same for a long time. Something was cracked, like a vase that had been repaired, but it wasn't quite the same. Did I want it to go further? No, I didn't.

'I have to thank you,' she said.

'For what?'

'For making me notice him.'

The shove came so hard, Adele lost her balance and landed on her arse on the floor. I collected my top off the floor and put it on.

'You are out of control and a terrible friend,' I spat at her.

'What? I'm doing you a favour,' she cried.

'I'm not a charity case,' I said curtly.

The front door opened and in came Alan in his usual leather jacket, jeans, hair styled to perfection, clear-eyed, no traces of a hangover on his handsome face. He glanced at Adele, who was on the floor.

'I see you're perky as usual,' he said sarcastically to me.

He helped Adele back on her feet and she buried her face in his neck as if he were a white knight.

I rolled my eyes.

'Where is the bathroom?' I asked.

'On the right, would you like a cup of tea?'

'Water,' I said, locating the bathroom.

In the bathroom, I peed and washed my face. It was a grey tiled room with a stone feature wall. There was a shelf with grey fluffy towels. I inspected the label, Ralph Lauren. I leaned against the sink and crossed my hands under my chest. Did Adele suggest we share him? Who would want to do that? If I had a man like him, I wouldn't want to share him with anyone. Adele knew I wouldn't ever take that offer; too proud. It was all or nothing with me. I would not settle for second best when I could be someone's best. Each time I thought the Adele I knew was back, she would ruin it by saying something like that. Adele was sitting on the sofa with her arms folded like a child who had been told off by an adult. I looked at the bookshelf. There were many books about the greatest composers: Chopin, Mozart, Beethoven, Bach etc. Alan stood by the counter eyeing me. Adele stood and stalked into another room, the bedroom I presumed.

'Can I have my phone now, please?' I said to him all businesslike.

'Of course,' he said, sliding it across the counter.

I took it and slipped it into the back pocket of my jeans. He passed me a glass of water.

'You look like you need it.'

I took it and tried not to gulp it down.

'How are you two friends?' he asked.

I licked my lips. 'We just are.'

'But how did you meet? You are so… different.'

'We're childhood friends, our parents are neighbours.'

'That grew apart,' he said.

I stared at him. 'We haven't grown apart.'

'No?' he said. 'There are too many cracks; I wonder what made it that way.'

'We have our differences like most friends do.'

'Sure, but I don't know… something is different between you two,' he said walking past me. 'I'd better check on her.'

I watched him go towards the bedroom. All I wanted to do was to lie down and sleep off this hangover. My stomach churned and my head pounded. I located my bag by the sofa and coat on the armchair by the bookshelf. I scanned the books again while putting my coat on. What an interesting choice of books. It would be nice to sit down and have an actual conversation with him, even though I knew nothing about composers. I was about to take a step forward when from the corner of my eye, I spotted a hardback with a black and white cover with squares that looked like tiles. I glanced towards the bedroom door. Voices were coming from behind it, but I couldn't make out what was being said. I tiptoed to the shelf and grabbed the book. Adele had the same book on her bedside table. *Lost and Found*. Nothing harmful about two people who were dating owning a copy of the same book, but what if this was much deeper than that? There had to be something I was missing. I adjusted the gap where the book was with another book hoping, Alan wouldn't notice then took off my coat, wrapped it around the book, and ran out of there.

Chapter Nine

When I woke up, it was getting dark out. I had slept for most of the afternoon. I went to the living room and stopped dead; the curtains were open again. Why did Adele keep doing this?

'Adele?' I called out.

Silence.

Adele must have come back to collect something, opened the curtains for an unknown reason, and left. I closed the curtains. The book was still wrapped in my coat. I made myself a cup of coffee and an omelette for dinner and read bits of the book. Nothing much happened in the first ten chapters, but by the eleventh chapter, Cody disappeared. A big search was conducted. The police questioned a woman named Melissa but nothing came out of that and the case went cold leaving Cody's family with no closure. With no body, there wasn't much the police could do. Three years had passed and Jenny, still haunted by her brother's disappearance continued her search for him. She looked on the internet but found nothing, then one day, while out shopping, she ran into Melissa. Jenny confronted her, but Melissa told her she didn't know what she wanted from her and had nothing to do with Cody's disappearance. Then the letter arrives. I stood up and went to the bedroom, engrossed by the entire plot. When Jenny reunited with her brother, he told her now that he had been found, he wanted Jenny to kill their mother and frame their father for her murder. The sound of the front door interrupted my reading.

Annoyed by this interruption, I shoved the book under the covers. I sat up straight and kept my eyes on the bedroom door. What if Alan found out the book was missing? I should have asked Adele if I could borrow hers instead of taking his. Knowing how watchful and guarded he was, Alan would notice. This made me quiver. Now, I faced another problem. How the hell I was going to smuggle the book into his apartment and put it back without him noticing? There were giggles and a door slammed. What Adele had told me that morning played on my mind. I could have him only if she were involved. A threesome. Her odd sexual behaviour bothered me. Adele had done nothing like that before, involving me in her sexual escapades. It was peculiar. She'd also had the nerve to thank me for her noticing him. She was doing this to tick me off. To make me snap.

Greg appeared before me in the hallway while I was on my way to class. He smiled down at me while I kept my face straight.

'Are you going to the party?' he asked.

'You know I don't do parties,' I said, walking past him.

He walked backwards. 'Oh, come on, Phoebe, it would be great.'

'Not interested.'

'Adele is coming with her new guy. I didn't know she had a new boyfriend.'

'Well, she does.'

'I will send you an invitation through Facebook,' he said and stalked off.

I stood in the corridor watching Greg and for a moment, I thought maybe I should give him a chance. What did I have to lose? My phone pinged with a notification. It was from Greg with the invitation to the party. Without thinking it through, I pressed on 'going'.

I bought cans of beer since it was a party. It was a suitable thing to do, not show up empty-handed. Adele wasn't in the apartment and she hadn't told me about the party so maybe she wasn't going. Alan must have had another engagement. Or they'd rather spend their time in bed than go to something so lame. Greg spotted me right away when I walked in. He waved at me and I threw him a cautious wave.

'You made it,' he said as if this was a mountain expedition.

'I have,' I said.

He awkwardly leaned forward to kiss me on both cheeks. From the corner of my eyes, I made out Adele lurking in the corner. She was dressed in a floral skater skirt so short her butt cheeks were almost on display. Alan was leaning on his side sipping on a bottle of beer, glancing nervously around the room. He did a double-take when he spotted me across the room and smiled. Janice and Hannah came in, Alan scowled at them and glanced away, his face going dark, and his jaw clenched. He seemed annoyed by Janice and Hannah. Why would he be? Did he know them? It was unlikely, but not impossible.

'So, what do you think?' Greg asked.

'About what?'

'The party.'

I glanced around at the people scattered in groups, drinking, talking, and smoking cigarettes. Music was playing on a playlist on Spotify. The room was foggy with smoke and there was a distinct smell in the air. Weed, I presumed.

'I think it's great,' I lied.

Adele said something to Alan and he smiled. Alan was right, Adele and I have grown apart and after graduation, we would go our separate ways. Or she would move out to live with Alan. Hannah and Janice were engrossed in their phones, then they said something to Adele. Alan kept looking away from Hannah and Janice until they left.

Greg and I talked about our studies. Adele didn't come to say hello. Still pissed at me for pushing her, I supposed. She'd had it coming, and I didn't regret it. The night went on; I didn't see Adele and Alan. Maybe they left.

There was this guy, Martin, who I used to see in the hall and we had classes together. He had blond curly hair, brown eyes, and crooked teeth. Nothing to write home about. Since we had classes together, we chatted. One day, he'd asked me if I'd like to go out with him for a drink. The drink led to sex in the back seat of his car. The whole thing was like a transaction.

'Would you like to do it?' he asked.

'Okay,' I said.

It wasn't like how it was in the movies, or what I read about in books. Nothing about it was measured and exact. It was awkward and clumsy. Zippers got stuck and teeth bumped together. The whole experience was cringe-worthy and painful. When it was over and Martin saw the blood, he freaked out.

'You should have said it was your first time,' he said.

'I…' I trailed off, my cheeks going red.

'Don't tell anyone okay that we…' he warned.

'Fine, I won't tell anyone,' I said.

I pulled my jeans on thinking, was that it? That was sex? The next day, in the halls, there was a picture of me with the word slut in red ink on the walls. Everyone stared at me and passed comments. It confused me since Martin had told me not to tell anyone. I didn't know why he would put a picture up and call me a slut when I was a virgin. A girl who I didn't know pushed me against the wall and told me to back off, Martin was her boyfriend. Adele stomped over, jumping to my defence, grabbing the girl by the shoulder pushing her against the wall.

'Fuck off! If you have an issue take it up with Martin. Leave her alone.' Adele spat at her.

I approached the situation with cold detachment. They thought I was a slut? Let them think what they wanted; I knew who I was. I swore after that day, I wouldn't get involved with anyone from my classes. So, there I was, breaking my rule as Greg pushed himself into me. As we lay in the grass, I looked up at the starless sky and the trees jerked with the soft ripple of the wind.

Chapter Ten

I avoided Greg for the rest of the morning. I didn't want to repeat the sex. It was something I wanted to erase from my memory. I ran into him in the halls and he gave me a look of dispassion and proceeded to his next lecture. I think he too realised it was a mistake.

I didn't tell Adele about it either and she wasn't around even if I wanted to tell her, but it was none of her business. I continued to read the book during a free lesson. The book ended with Jenny killing her brother as she couldn't bring herself to kill her mother and frame her father for the murder so Cody would come back home. Since he was already missing, Jenny got away with killing her brother. The ending depressed me and left me sad and confused. Cody had planned to go missing, did it for attention, and was playing a game with his sister. What was the connection with Alan I wanted to know? Why did Adele have this book as well?

I arrived home around six, and all I wanted was to do a bit of bookkeeping, cook dinner, study, watch a bit of TV and have an early night. I took a deep breath as I always do before I opened the door. Adele didn't seem to be home. The closer she got to Alan, the further she drifted from me. I placed my bag down and the curtains were open again. I huffed and closed them. Giggles came from

Adele's room. So, she was home with him. I surveyed the state the apartment was in. Her shit was everywhere and I mean everywhere. A stocking dangling on the lamp, a jacket on the sofa, a skirt on the floor. A pile of clothes in the corner. How could I allow myself to live under these conditions? I contributed more than she did. So, she ironed the clothes when she felt like it, so what? I went to the kitchen. Dirty glasses were on the sink. I patiently washed a glass and opened the fridge. Her clutch bag was on the top shelf. Who leaves a clutch bag in the bloody fridge? Seeing that bag in there was like someone had poured gasoline and lit a match. How dare she? Truly, how dare she? Who did Adele think she was, taking me for granted like this? Leaving a mess everywhere and I clean up her shit like a bloody servant. Not only that, I had to listen to her getting fucked by Alan. This was a nightmare. Enough was enough. I had been quiet for too long. Adele had taken this a step too far. I marched to her room, clutching her bag so hard my knuckles were white. I opened the door without knocking, not caring if they were naked; they weren't. I threw the bag at Adele and it hit her on the forehead.

'What the fuck!' Adele yelled.

'No, no, you don't get to yell.'

Alan was too shocked to speak. My eyes passed through him. This was all because of him. One man. If I hadn't laid eyes on him, none of this would have happened. But if it wasn't him, it would be someone else. It was too hard to keep my cool, but I spoke to him in a steady voice.

'I have to talk to her. Alone.'

'No, he stays,' Adele shouted.

I grabbed a cardigan from the floor and threw it at her; it landed on her face. She kicked her feet on the bed and if I wasn't so angry, I would have laughed. The whole thing was ridiculous and juvenile. Alan would not stand there and watch us bicker like two crazy bitches. He stomped past me without saying a word, slamming the front door so hard, it rattled the whole flat. I left Adele's bedroom and collected her clothes. Adele was screaming obscenities at me and I returned holding a large bundle of clothes and threw it at her. She screamed.

'We need to discuss some house rules,' I said.

'Fuck you,' she spat, tears streaming down her face. 'You just ruined everything.'

'Then you'll fix it later! This place is a mess. I can't live like this anymore, cleaning up after your shit. All you do is get fucked by *him*.'

Adele's eyes narrowed at me. 'Oh, I see what this is all about? Ever since I told you I'm seeing him, you went all distant, cold, and shit. He's fucking me, not you. Get over it! As if a guy like Alan would be interested in you. You're like wood. Cold as stone.'

'It's either wood or a stone, Adele, I can't be both, but I don't think Alan is with you because of your high IQ,' I spat at her.

'At least I'm not sexless and unfuckable.'

We yelled and shouted, letting Alan win. Not believing we were stooping this low. We were too good for this. A guy winning over a long-term friendship. Adele's head was too far into her arse to realise what was happening. She was crazy about him. Walk straight into the wall kind of infatuation. Obsessed. Blind. It was so sad that our friendship would end like this, but I didn't want it to end, I wanted to work things out. To come to some sort of terms, to make her see how unreasonable she was being.

'I get him to notice you through me,' she said.

'Am I supposed to thank you? Is that what you're trying to tell me?'

'That's exactly what I'm telling you. I offered you an alternative if you want him so bad, but you wouldn't take it. You are too selfish.'

'By sharing him? What is he? A platter? And I don't want him. The pair of you can go and get fucked.'

She jumped off the bed. 'I can't talk to you when you're like this.'

'Look,' I said. 'I just want to work out—'

'Fuck off and die!' she spat.

'If that's how you want to play it, you narcissistic bitch, why don't you fuck off and die,' I said.

She looked at me as if I'd punched her.

'Well, at least I'm not boring.' she said, marching past me to the living room and slamming the front door behind her.

My chest rose and fell as if I'd run a marathon. I padded to the bathroom and washed my face with cold water, resting both of my hands on the sink. I levelled my breathing. Okay, it blew out of proportion, we fought, friends fight, it's normal. She'd come around. This wasn't the end of our friendship. I opened the medicine cabinet and spotted the sleeping pills. I popped three pills in my mouth and lay on the sofa trying to sleep this horrible night off.

There was pounding coming from somewhere, in my head most probably, but it became more demanding, more insistent. A groan came from somewhere. It was coming from me. A key in the door now, I opened my eyes; all I saw were clouds. The front door opened and a shape appeared. A woman. Adele had come back to pack her shit most likely, but she couldn't just leave, not until we talked about this and worked out this misunderstanding.

'Phoebe.'

My vision cleared.

'You're all over the place,' the voice said.

It wasn't Adele, but Alan. Where did he get the key? It had to be Adele of course; she would give him a key to allow him more access into our lives, coming in and out whenever he wanted. He was crouching by my side, shaking me. I sat up and frowned as I found myself on the floor. How did I end up there? All I remembered was lying on the sofa. I must have fallen asleep and fell off the sofa and I was so doped out from the sleeping pills, I didn't even notice. I rubbed my forehead. My brain swam. Alan stood and was inspecting the sleeping pills, which were on the coffee table. How did they get there? Did I carry them with me? Why couldn't I remember? What was happening to me?

'Jesus,' he muttered, 'how many did you take?'

'I don't know two, three maybe,' I said standing up and almost toppling but just keeping my balance.

'You're not sure? How come you're not in a coma?

'I wish I was,' I said.

Adele had stormed out and by the looks of it, she hadn't come back yet. Where was she? Where did she go? Why was Alan here? I poured myself a glass of water. Alan looked at me with both concern and disapproval.

'Where is Adele?' he asked.

The question felt like a knife slicing through the air. The room felt cold. Where was Adele? I didn't know where she was. Wouldn't she go crying to him? Why was he here? I drank my water, washing the foul metallic taste from my mouth. If he was here, and Adele didn't go to him, then where did she go? My heart sank.

'I thought she was with you,' I said.

'Well, clearly she isn't. I wouldn't be here otherwise,' he said drily.

'Of course, you wouldn't,' I snapped.

He rubbed his jaw. 'Look, I didn't see her last night after I left. She didn't come back here at all?'

'No,' I said. 'I don't think so.'

'You don't think so?' he asked, raising his voice and I couldn't stand it. 'You have to be sure.'

'I don't know what you want from me? I don't know where she is.'

'What did you do with my girlfriend?' he shouted. 'Where is she? What have you done with her?'

I placed my hand over my banging head. I couldn't take it, this shouting, it was giving me a headache. I wanted to cry but couldn't. His words sank in. What did I do with his girlfriend? What have I done with her? Did he think I did something to Adele? He was glaring at me, everything about him stiff and cold.

'Done with her? Do you think I did something to Adele? Look, we argued and she stormed out I thought she went to you.'

'Phoebe, you've been nothing but shit to her,' he said.

Me, a shit friend? What she had been saying to Alan? Was she trying to play the victim? To make me look bad? I slammed the glass down, inflamed by those accusations. I couldn't take it out on him, he was the caring boyfriend worried about the welfare of his girlfriend. Somehow, I couldn't keep calm.

'Oh, I'm the shit friend?' I shouted. 'Why am I always perceived as the arsehole? She's the bitch, not me. Stop seeing her as this perfect princess. Sorry to break it to you, mate, but her shit doesn't smell of roses,' I retorted.

'Cast your differences aside for one second and look at the bigger picture,' he said through gritted teeth. 'If she didn't come here and she didn't come to my place either, then where the hell is she? I tried calling her but all of my calls went through to voicemail.'

'We fought, Alan. You want to know what about? You. She's upset and I'm upset as you can see. Maybe she went to cool off somewhere and switched off her phone. She'll come around in her own time.'

He took a step closer to me, desperation in his eyes, 'You know her better than I do. Has she done this before? Taken off, not telling anyone, not answering her phone?'

I glanced at my feet. No, she never took off, it was unlike her to do something like this.

'No… but the fight we had was…'

Childish, that was what it was. 'We never fought like that before,' I said. 'Did you check if she's at Hannah and Janice's?'

'They haven't seen her either,' he said and ran his hand through his hair. 'If she gets in touch with you, let me know, *immediately*.'

I nodded; he turned and left.

Chapter Eleven

Hours passed and no word from Adele. I tried calling her, but the calls went straight to voicemail. I checked her activity on Facebook. The last time she had been active on there was twelve hours ago, that was before we argued. I checked her Facebook feed; the last post she'd made was three days ago, where she shared a video of a cat playing. She'd come around, I kept telling myself. She would walk through the door. I called her parents. Adele wasn't there either. I would not notify the police yet.

I spent the day cleaning the apartment, washing the dishes, dusting, and cleaning the bathroom. I didn't touch Adele's room. Her mess, she could deal with it. I looked out the window and saw Alan sitting on the sofa holding his phone. I shut the curtains and turned, facing the clock on the wall. Its hands were on 9:00. It had stopped working. To give myself something to do, I adjusted it.

The buzzer went off a few hours later; it was odd to hear it as it hardly ever rang. We weren't much into having visitors. It was Marion, Adele's mother.

'Have you heard from Adele yet? That is why you called right?' she demanded. 'Is she here?'

I shook my head and opened the door wider for her to come in. At least the place was clean. If she'd seen it hours before, she would have been horrified.

'No, she's not,' I said.

'What do you mean she's not here, where is she?'

I would not mention the fight.

'Did she tell you where she was going?' Marion asked.

'No, she didn't. I thought she went to see Alan.'

'Alan who?' she asked.

So, Adele didn't tell her parents about the new stunning addition in her life.

'A guy she's been dating for a few months.'

'And she didn't bother to tell me?'

'I…'

'It's not your fault. If you hear from her please, call me.'

'I will,' I said.

'I'm so worried, it's so unlike her to take off not answering her phone. After you called, I tried calling her and she didn't pick up then I got a call from her work. She was supposed to fill in for a girl today and didn't show up. Her manager tried to call her but the call went to voicemail so he called me.'

'Did you call the police?' I asked.

'Yes, dear, I have, but they said there was nothing they could do as she could come back and hadn't been gone for twenty-four hours yet. Can you believe it? Anything can happen in twenty-four hours!'

'I'll let you know if I hear something.' I said.

Alan showed up again, knocking this time, and I let him in. He looked distraught and worried. He truly cared for Adele, when all she cared about was what was between his legs. He walked past me and scanned the apartment as if I was holding Adele captive in a secret room. He looked at me and I shook my head. I went to the kitchen and poured two glasses of wine. He stood there with his hands on his hips peering at the empty pizza box on the coffee table, beside a mug of coffee and a glass of wine; the TV was on an episode of *Friends*.

'You don't look like you were scuttling around the city looking for her,' he said.

'And by doing that, do you think I would find her?' I said and looked him up and down. 'You're not running all over London looking for her either.'

'How can you be so relaxed when your friend goes missing?' he asked, ignoring my question.

'I am not relaxed, all right. She's not missing, Alan, she's only seeking attention. She's a selfish person,' I said, handing him a glass of wine and walked past him.

'She was right, you are cold,' he said.

I sat on the sofa. 'She's talked about me with you?'

'Of course, she has.'

'That's not a sexy conversation to have in bed,' I remarked.

'She said you have a crush on me. She made fun of you because of that.'

'You know she's using you, right? When she's busy making fun of me with you, Adele told me, she's not interested in you as a person, but for what you can give her, what you can do for her,' I said.

He looked hurt.

'What did you think?' I went on plunging the knife deeper. It was my turn to hurt him, to twist the blade and let him bleed dry.

'That it was going to be Sunday lunches, tea with lemon cakes, and holding hands like a respectable couple.'

'Your friend is nowhere to be found, get some perspective,' he said.

'And you're a fool for thinking it was going to last. I know Adele better than anyone, as you said. You are temporary until something better comes along. It's all happened before. You fell for the wrong woman.'

He walked towards me, placing the glass of wine gently on the coffee table.

'Oh, really? And you think you are the right woman for me? With Sunday lunches, as you put it. Tea with lemon cakes and holding hands like a respectable couple? You and your sex appeal of a dead slug?'

Ouch. That hurt. I wasn't Adele. I wasn't a girly girl that would make his brain turn pink. I didn't wear thongs with matching bras. I mean, who has time for that shit, anyway? I didn't have nail extensions with exotic colours, wear exaggerated high heels, and miniskirts. I was a simple woman with poker-straight black hair, thick eyebrows, and plump lips. I wore conservative clothes, I had bare nails, wore flats, and cotton panties. Comfort over everything.

'I thought you were smarter,' I said.

'I'm going to ask you again,' Alan said, 'Did you do something to Adele?'

I coughed. 'What are you getting at?'

'You were furious, maybe things got out of hand.'

'Yes, I was angry. What you think I did? Kill her and hide her body? Do you know how preposterous that sounds?'

'If she calls you, be sure to call me, right away.'

Chapter Twelve

I went into Adele's room; it was the same as I'd left it, with the explosion of clothes. The book *Lost and Found* was still on the bedside table. I left her room, turned, and stopped dead. The cuckoo clock had stopped working again. The apartment felt cold, as if its temperature had dropped. I put the kettle on and the buzzer went off, making me jump, and I dropped the mug on the floor. It smashed as it hit the marble. I cleaned up the broken pieces as fast as I could and went to the buzzer. On the screen was a man and a woman.

'Yes?' I said.

'Phoebe Kelsey?' the man said.

'Yes.'

'This is DS Williams and DC Nash; we would like to ask you a few questions regarding Adele Graham,' the man said.

I stared at the tiny screen as they showed me their badges, which I couldn't read. I buzzed them in and lingered by the front door. The woman had curly hair, tall with brown skin, and the man was slightly younger with his hair too short, hooded eyes, and a hooked nose. I spotted a wedding ring on his finger and he was gaining weight in the middle. They showed me their badges again.

'We would like to ask you a few questions, do you mind if we come in?' DC Nash said.

They looked around before they sat on the sofa. I sat across from them. Nash took out a notepad from her inner jacket pocket while Williams had his phone ready. Old-fashioned versus the new.

'For how long did you know Adele?' Nash began.

I noticed how she referred to Adele in the past tense, not in the present. As if she was presuming the worst. Lost hope before it even started.

'Since childhood,' I said.

'So, you are close?' Williams said.

'We are.'

'And you've shared this flat for how long?' Nash asked.

'Since we started uni.'

One scribbled down notes, the other tapped away on his phone.

'In these past few weeks, did Adele mention anything about going away or have you noticed anything unusual in her behaviour?' Nash went on.

I shook my head.

'What is that, Ms Kelsey?'

'No, I haven't.'

'When was the last time you saw Adele?'

'In here, she and Alan were here.'

'Alan is her boyfriend?' Williams asked.

'Yes.'

'How long has Adele been dating him?'

'About three months.'

'And how would you describe their relationship?'

The questions were like a never-ending machine gun. In these cases, it's always the boyfriend or the husband who's a prime suspect. Did Alan have something to do with Adele's disappearance? He came into the picture and Adele vanishes, telling no one where she was going when it's not like her at all. Now the police were taking this seriously and a grip like iron squeezed my heart. We had our differences, but I wouldn't wish any harm to her. The two officers stared at me, waiting for an answer. How would I describe their relationship? I didn't know, I couldn't find the words. Nash raised her eyebrows at me, and Williams gaped at me. Both waiting.

'They're into each other,' I said, blurting the first words that sprang to mind.

'Did Adele show any signs of mistreatment?'

Was Adele being mistreated by Alan? Ridiculous. She adored him, and he worshipped her. At least that was the front they displayed.

'No,' I said.

'So, the last time you saw Adele was here at this apartment?' Williams asked again to clarify.

'Yes.'

'What time was that?'

'Around… ten.'

'In the evening?'

'Yes, in the evening.'

'And then what happened?' Nash asked.

'What do you mean?'

'You saw her at ten pm, did Adele tell you she was going somewhere?'

The image of Adele storming out came before me. I would not mention we'd had a row; better to leave that out. What if they spoke to Alan and he told them? They must have spoken to him first. My nails bit into my palm in sharp crescents and my knuckles thrust through the red of my skin.

'She didn't say.'

'Was there anything unusual in her manner?'

'No,' I said.

Yet everything was so unusual about how she'd behaved. Making a pass at me, telling me I could have Alan only if she joined in.

Williams stared at me. 'What about you?'

I looked at him; I didn't understand his question, so I gave him no answer.

'Did you stay here or go somewhere?' Nash asked.

The memory came of me popping the sleeping pills.

'I went to bed,' I said.

They glanced at each other. I didn't like this one bit. Williams glanced at me before he tapped on his phone.

'Is there someone who can vouch you were here?'

What was this? Did they think I—?

'No,' I said. 'But there are cameras on the premises. If you look at the CCTV, they'll show I stayed here throughout the night,' I said confidently, unlike how I felt.

What if the CCTV showed something else? What if Adele came back here and left while I was out cold?

Nash shut the notebook, which made me jump a little. 'Where is her room?'

'On the left.'

'Do you mind if I look?' Williams asked.

Shouldn't they have a warrant for that? I let him through so I wouldn't appear difficult or as though I had something to hide.

Williams stood and went to Adele's room. It was all too surreal.

'Is Adele listed as "missing"?' I asked.

'Nothing is certain. Her mother made a report. Usually, the person will turn up, but Adele has already been missing for over twenty-four hours,' Nash pointed out. 'Why didn't you report her as missing?'

The question threw me off guard.

'I thought she went away.'

'Did she tell you she was going away?'

'No.'

'And has she taken off in the past?'

'No.'

'Can you tell me what Adele was wearing?'

What was Adele wearing? I didn't remember.

'Jeans and a jumper,' I said.

'What colour was her jumper?'

I couldn't be sure. Was it white or pink? No, pink.

'Pink and light blue jeans,' I said.

I didn't like the way Nash looked at me one bit. I had this creeping feeling nagging at me that I was in deep shit.

Chapter Thirteen

The apartment was like a museum with people coming in and going. The police came with a warrant this time to search the apartment. Journalists gathered outside. I still couldn't fathom it; Adele classified as a missing person. My mum came over with my dad and Tom.

'Oh, honey,' Mum said, enveloping me in a hug. 'I'm so sorry, everyone is so shocked.'

Somehow hearing my mum saying this made it all much worse.

'How has this happened?' Mum asked.

And there it was: the questions. They came one by one. Questions I have answered time and time again.

'Adele wouldn't just take off,' Dad said.

Adele did take off, however, and it was selfish of her to do this to her parents. To put all of us in this position. Adele's parents came over, asking me the same questions as my parents, and as the police did. Her mother blamed me. I could see it in her eyes. The judgement that I should have notified the police right away and there would have been the chance of finding her. I was the bitch who let her daughter go missing. I didn't tell my parents or Adele's about the fight either. It was better to leave it out or they would think I triggered it. I might have. I was to blame, I was too harsh on her. I didn't think Alan had told anyone about the fight either if he had, the police would have questioned me about it. Why hadn't he told them about the argument?

'Why don't you come and stay with us for a few days?' Mum suggested.

The police wanted us to stay in the kitchen and didn't let us go anywhere else. This was my apartment and I wasn't allowed to move freely in it.

'I'd better stay here. Just in case she comes back, I want to be here.'

'If the police let you stay here,' Tom said in a low tone.

'Why wouldn't they?' I asked.

'Because this is the last place she was seen in.'

'What about this new boyfriend, what do you know about him?' Dad asked.

'He's a new guy she had been seeing,' I said.

'Yes, but what do you know about him?' Mum asked.

I looked at Tom and I wondered how much he told my parents.

'Adele has seen plenty of guys before but never disappeared,' Tom remarked.

What was he saying; that Alan did something to her? Did he?

'I'm sure there is a reasonable explanation for everything,' I said.

'I'll stay with you for a few days,' Tom said.

'That won't be necessary,' I said.

'I wasn't asking,' Tom said.

'I don't think you should stay here all by yourself. Having Tom here for a few days is a good idea,' Dad said.

I relented and let Tom stay with me.

I took time off from university and work. I needed to figure out what was going on. I wouldn't be able to take it either, to have all those eyes on me. Like Adele's mother, judging me. That I was to blame. It was my fault. The police asked more questions and I gave them the same answers. The CCTV cameras in the apartment and on the street showed Adele coming out of our apartment and crossing the street to Alan's apartment. She rang the buzzer. Lover boy didn't give her a key, it seemed. When no one answered, she didn't come back here but took the route to the right. I knew because Nash asked if I knew anything about where Adele was heading. It didn't show *me* on the cameras which I thought was a good thing.

Adele's laptop was taken away. The police checked her bag and all she had taken with her was her phone and cash, nothing else. Her passport was still in the drawer, so she didn't flee the country. Where was she? Where could Adele have gone? Where could she go with just her phone and money?

People went missing, 180,000 of them, some of whom are children. A few were found. A few came back. There were mentions of Adele's disappearance in the newspapers. Seeing her name made it unreal. It was stuff that happened to other people. The tragedies of life where you read about them in the papers, or watch it on the news but being part of it, made it unsettling.

I went on Adele's Facebook; there were a few messages from people who knew Adele telling her to come home. Others wished she was well wherever she was. As if she was going to read these messages. The thing was, Adele wasn't the sort of person to go missing on her own accord. I knew her well enough to know she wouldn't plan to do something like this. What if she went to a bar and met someone who turned out to be a lunatic and did something terrible to her?

'I think the Alan guy had something to do with it,' Tom said during dinner. 'I checked and there is no record about this guy whatsoever, it's strange.'

Did Tom look Alan up? How did he find out his second name?

'You looked him up?' I asked.

'Yes, I got curious after what you told me.'

'How did you know his last name?'

'You told me.'

Did I? I didn't recall.

'It's strange and you mentioned this to Adele and she didn't bother with it. She got what she deserved for being stupid.'

'Tom!' I exclaimed. 'That's an awful thing to say.'

'I feel bad she's missing but let's not pretend she's a saint either.'

'No, she wasn't. I don't think Alan had anything to do with it though. He was out that night, he had alibis.'

'He could have hired someone to do the work for him.'

'Why would he do that? Under what motive?'

'I don't know. You weren't in bed with them so you didn't know what was going on behind the scenes.'

I pushed my plate aside, the entire conversation had lost me the little appetite I had. I rubbed my scalp, massaging it to relieve the stress weighing down on me.

'They were together for only three months. In those stages the relationship would still be in its full bloom,' I said.

The buzzer went off— a sound that had become customary now. I stood to answer the door, relieved by the interruption. It was Janice. She was alone, which was strange to see, since Janice and Hannah always came in a pair, like earrings. She was dressed in a red coat with a thick woollen scarf wrapped around her neck. Her blonde hair was up in a messy bun.

'I thought I'd come by to see how you're doing,' she said.

Touched by her thoughtfulness, I opened the door wider for her to come in. As she walked past me, a strong but feminine perfume danced within my nose. Tom was clearing the plates and Janice stopped dead.

'Oh, I didn't know you had a guest,' she said, checking him out.

'This is my brother, Tom. Tom, this Adele's friend, Janice.'

Tom gave Janice a friendly wave. I offered Janice something to drink but she shook her head as she settled down on the sofa.

'It's all been... shocking,' she whispered. 'How could Adele just take off? I mean, she would have told us if she planned to go somewhere.'

'Us?' I asked.

'Hannah and I.'

'I don't know it's... stressful.'

'I can imagine this is hard on you, given you live together and Adele is difficult to live with, you know how she is.'

Tom was busying himself with the dishes and I wondered how much he could hear.

'When was the last time you spoke to her?'

'That morning, she had classes as you know.'

I nodded. 'Did the police speak to you?'

Janice looked at me as if I'd asked something odd. 'Yes, they have.'

'What did they say?'

'They asked me about her behaviour, her manner, about her relationship with Alan.'

'What did you say?'

Janice sighed and tilted her head back. 'That Adele was fine, nothing was off about her. Didn't look like she was going to disappear and from what Adele said about Alan, she seemed really into him.'

'You and Hannah were with her and Alan at the party,' I pointed out.

'Yes, you saw us.'

'Was it there you met him for the first time?'

There was a hesitation. 'Yes.'

Did Adele tell Hannah and Janice I had a crush on him? I suppose she did and made fun of me as she did with Alan.

'Anyway,' she said standing, 'I'd better leave you to it.'

'It was nice of you to come.'

She nodded. 'Um… can you not mention I came here,' she said, 'to anyone.'

I blinked at her.

'Can you?' she asked, her eyes going to Tom.

'I wasn't going to,' I replied.

'Good.'

When Tom left three days later, I went to Adele's room. The police had already searched and taken whatever they found useful but I looked, just in case. I opened drawers and the closet. Looking at her clothes, shoes, bags, makeup. Did Adele use all of this? We own so much shit and we only use a quarter of it. Who needs all those shoes for a pair of feet, all those clothes for just one body?

I sat on the bed, the same bed where we used to lie and talk for hours. Now, there will be no more of that. I would never hear her laugh. I didn't have to wash dirty glasses after her. Why was I thinking of her as if Adele would never be found? She was missing, not dead. Adele would come back. Adele *had* to come back. Adele *will* come back. The copy of *Lost and Found* lay on the bedside table. I went to my room, took the book I had taken from Alan and placed them side by side. I didn't know what I was looking for. They were identical but, why shouldn't they be? Both the same edition authored by Robert Freeman. I did a quick Google search on my phone; there was a Goodreads page, and the book had a handful of reviews, mostly five stars. There was no picture of the author. On the bio was the date of birth, and what he liked to do when he wasn't writing, nothing else. There was the Amazon page with no picture either and hardly any info, and it was the only book the author had published.

Didn't the police think it was suspicious that Adele had a copy of a book about a character who went missing and then she disappeared? It was a bit of a coincidence. But the police would not build a case based on a work of fiction. They relied on facts. People read crime all the time, it didn't make them serial killers or about to plot a murder. I placed her book back where it was and carried Alan's copy with me to the living room. That hole in my stomach nudged at me. I was missing something, and the answer might be in front of me and I was failing to see it. What if the book was connected to all of this? What if something deeper and more sinister lay within? I saw this gorgeous guy named Alan and Adele went after him. She started dating him or sleeping with him, whatever it may be. She had a book about a brother going missing who was found by his sister. Alan had the same book. Was Tom right? Was Alan connected to this somehow?

I dragged my feet to the window and opened the curtain, Alan was home. How could this have happened?

How could I allow this to happen? A scream came out of me and the book went flying, hitting the wall, and fell on the floor. I screamed again, burning my throat. I crouched into a ball on the floor and burst into tears. A new nightmare had emerged. First, it was Adele with Alan. Then she had gone missing. The sobs made my entire body heave, making it difficult to breathe.

I was spread across the floor, too weak to move, too powerless to do anything. There was a key in the lock, I was too exhausted to see if it was in my head or someone was getting in. A pair of boots appeared. The sight of them didn't startle me. Alan came to view. He'd used the key Adele had given him. I didn't tell him to give me the key back, I just stared at him. Studying his beautiful face, looking deeply into his blue eyes. He scooped me off the floor. I groaned as if I were in agony and buried my face on his neck, inhaling in his scent. The cigarettes, beer, and the aquatic, fresh perfume. He located my bedroom and tucked me into bed as if I were a helpless baby. Like a parent taking a child to bed. I'd never had a man in my room. It was my domain, pure, clean from men. Now he'd invaded that too.

'Did you tell the police... that Adele and I...'

'Shh....' he cooed lying over me on the bed running his hand through my hair. It felt strangely intimate and something inside me jolted awake, sending spasms of electricity into me.

'Don't think about that now. But no, I haven't told them anything,' he whispered.

And I lay there wondering why. Why on earth he didn't tell the police? This was my fault.

In the morning, I woke up to find Alan sleeping in the armchair. I watched him for a while, taking him in. Adele was gone and he was here in my bedroom asleep in my armchair. He shouldn't be here.

Alan stirred and I shut my eyes and kept my breathing level as if I were asleep. I heard him stand and pace out of the room. I remembered throwing his hardback in the middle of the room. What if he saw it? Perhaps he already had. Did he creep around the apartment in the dark while I was asleep? He had been here many times before, but the idea of him creeping in the dark without Adele didn't sit well with me. I stood from the bed, the floor cold under my bare feet then yawned and went to the living room. It was strange to see him in the kitchen. Did he look around while he was here with Adele? What did she show him? Identifying what was hers and what was mine. He glared at me and that weird, electric sensation returned, spooling all over me. People like Adele and Alan had no idea what it was like to be lonely. They think they know but they only know about the last time they had been single and endured a month of loneliness before meeting someone new. They didn't know about the lonely weekends spent on your own because you had only a few friends and they had plans of their own. You read a book or two from cover to cover. How each book you owned was actually read, not sitting on the shelf for decoration. They didn't know what it was like to be so chronically untouched that an accidental brush with a stranger sent sparks of longing to your groin. To look blankly out of the window gazing at nothing in particular and say to yourself, *I just can't bear it anymore.* Loneliness can be a prison.

I didn't look at where the book lay face down. Alan would look at where I was looking. Did he notice his book had gone missing? If he did, he would assume it was me who took it, then why had he mentioned nothing? It was hardly the time, a missing book from its shelf was nothing compared to a missing girlfriend. As I stood there, a memory of Adele came to me when she came with me to do some undergarment shopping. It was strange and somewhat funny how this came to me now. I picked the five-packs of briefs, safe, practical, and comfortable. Adele shrugged and told me.

'Can't you wear something nice for once in your life?'

'They're cute,' I protested.

'If your idea of cute is of parachutes, sure,' she said disapprovingly.

'They are not,' I said. 'Besides, I have no man to wear them for.'

'It's not for a man,' she said rolling her eyes. 'It's for you, how confident you feel knowing that underneath your clothes, you're wearing something sexy and hot, daring even,' she told me in her sultry voice. 'And yes, if a guy does come along, you'd be all nice and prepared.'

Adele was all about being nice and prepared for that *just in case* encounter. I on the other hand didn't have encounters, I didn't have escorts either. I knew this and she knew it. She had tried to get me out of my introverted shell, but each time I went out with her to clubs, I ended up being bored to tears. So, I stayed with my comfortable cotton undies. If a man came along, he would make do with what he had, he'd just tear them off either way, so what's the point? Because men are visual creatures, as if women aren't. I haven't seen men going out of their way either. Then it hit me again. There would be no more underwear shopping now, and no Adele to scold me about my horrendous choice of undergarments.

'Did you stay the night?' I asked as if I weren't aware.

Alan sighed and shut his eyes, and his long eyelashes kissed his cheek. 'Yes. I slept in the armchair.'

'Why?'

'I was worried… the last thing I need is for you to do… something,' he said.

What did he think I was going to do? Hurt myself? I was upset, that was all. It was normal given the situation. The kettle boiled and Alan made coffee, or attempted to. He stopped halfway through this task and ran his hand over his forehead and huffed.

'I don't know how you like your coffee. I haven't asked if you like coffee or tea? And I'm in your kitchen.' He cast me a shy look. 'You seem like a coffee person.' He lowered his eyes beneath his long eyelashes.

'I like coffee, black and bitter like my soul,' I said.

He chuckled. At least I made him smile. Did Adele make him laugh?

He went on making the coffee while I strode towards the wall unit, turned my back to him and picked up the book. I opened the drawer and placed it there to deal with later. We sat across from each other, silently sipping our coffee.

'How are you?' he said quietly.

'I've been better,' I said.

He rubbed his temples. 'I'm sorry, that was a stupid question.'

'No, it wasn't,' I said, a little too fast. 'It's fine... I haven't been asked that question in a long time.' I glanced at the black liquid in my mug. 'How are you?' I asked.

'Same... I've been better. You can't be prepared for something like this. Nothing prepares you for something this... awful. I am going out of my mind thinking of a place where she could have gone, thinking of something she mentioned but... I...' he trailed off, lowering his head.

He loved her and Adele didn't give a damn about him. At least, that was the impression she'd given. Alan was good looking, foxy even, and that was what Adele saw: a man who was her equal so to speak. That was supposed to be the moment where I placed my hand on his and provided comfort, said the right words, but I didn't have any right words to say because as Alan said nothing prepares you for something so awful. Life didn't come with an instruction manual on how to deal with someone disappearing, or worse, someone getting killed. The buzzer shrieked which made us both jump. We looked at each other. Alan checked his watch.

'Are you expecting someone?' he asked.

I shook my head. 'I'd better check.'

There was a knock on the door. Someone must have gone out, and the person buzzing got in.

'Can I use your bathroom?' he asked.

Why he was being so formal? I'd heard him give Adele orgasms. We were way past any forms of pleasantries.

'Sure,' I said.

I went to the door and before me stood DC Nash.

Chapter Fourteen

'Good morning,' Nash said.

She was alone today. 'I have a few more questions, shall we?'

She was business-like as usual; I didn't think she would ask me if I had a good night's sleep and she didn't apologise for coming so early. It was past nine o'clock so hardly early, but for Alan it was. He'd said once, he didn't like to wake until two pm and I wondered if he worked as he claimed. Nash looked around the apartment and her eyes lingered on the two empty mugs on the kitchen counter. She knew I had company but didn't ask if this was the right time. It wasn't. Alan was there, and I thought of locking him in the bathroom and urging him to be quiet. This wouldn't look good, the boyfriend and the best friend together. My heart pumped and I had to sit on the sofa with the fear I would faint. The bathroom door opened and Alan came out, stopping dead at the sight of Nash with a notebook ready in hand. Her eyes were hard. She thought we were fucking. It was that simple. Why would he be here otherwise? Now, she would build a theory that Alan and I were into each other, having an affair most probably, and it got so intense and passionate between us we had to get rid of Adele so we could be together. My thoughts were running away with me, making my head spin. She couldn't arrest us based on theories and suspicions. Nash raised an eyebrow at me and pointed her pen at me and him.

'Are you two close?'

The translation to this was clear: Are you two fucking?

'We hang out together... I mean with Adele,' I said.

Another eyebrow raise. That came out wrong. Now she would think Adele and I were sharing him. Alan sat on the sofa far away from me as if this would prove to Nash that no, we weren't fucking. I have the sex appeal of a dead slug. I didn't have a golden cunt where he could sink his precious gilded cock into. I was a slug. Slimy and disgusting. The unwelcomed little creature; he wouldn't touch me with a six-foot pole.

'Phoebe used to join us for drinks sometimes,' he said.

That was how I should have answered. Cool and collected. He was like a cat, this Alan, pretty, watchful, alert, and guarded.

'I see,' Nash said. 'The reason I'm here is that a neighbour came forward and claimed he heard shouting coming from this apartment the night Adele went missing. What can you tell me about that?'

Oh shit, shit, shit. I opened my mouth and closed it. I couldn't glance at Alan or Nash would know something was up. We were loud that night. I was surprised the whole block didn't hear us shouting, calling each other obscenities. I wanted to ask what the neighbour heard exactly, but Alan chimed in.

'We were shouting,' he admitted.

Nash leaned in, interested. 'What about?'

'Adele and I were in her room and Phoebe came in.'

He was going to sell me out. I could hear it, the bus coming and him throwing me under it. I stayed with my hands clasped on my lap, unable to move. I couldn't cross my arms, that would come across as defensive.

'And?'

'We were shouting because of a joke.'

'A joke?' Nash said, lifting an eyebrow.

'We liked to play around and Phoebe was teasing Adele because she left a mess everywhere, weren't you, Phoebe?' he asked.

I stared at him with my mouth gaping open.

'We were, yes.'

'The neighbour said you were calling each other names.'

'We were,' I said, now playing the game. What was he on about? Why was he lying to the police?'

'We're practical jokers,' Alan said.

She stared at us. Did Nash buy into our bullshit? I doubted it. She sighed, shut the notebook and stood.

'Thank you for your time,' she said, passing another judgemental look at us before leaving.

All I could do was stare at the front door after I'd shown her out. Why was Alan covering my arse?

His eyes were hot on me. My face was devoid of colour.

'You look like you need to lie down,' he said taking my hand and guiding me to the sofa.

Was he this attentive with Adele? He leaned on the sofa, arm across from me.

'Did you just lie to Nash for me?'

'Yes,' he said casually. As if I asked him if he bought milk.

'Why? Why didn't you tell her the truth? Why didn't you tell her we argued when they came to question you?'

'Because it would have reflected badly on you.'

'So what? Why should you care? I'm the bitch who drove your girlfriend to go missing, you should hate me, not be covering for me.'

He sighed as if he was dealing with a complicated child.

'It's not your fault Adele went missing.'

'Yes, it is.'

'Listen to me for a second here, okay,' he snapped. 'You were pissed off. You found me here with Adele, which made you angrier. You fought, she stormed out and never returned home. Do you know how that would make you look? It's normal for friends to fight, but not when the police are involved. They would think you have something to do with her disappearance. Which you didn't.'

'You're the first one accused me of having done something.'

'I was upset. I didn't mean it.' He checked his watch. 'I have to go, I'll drop by later, okay?'

'Why?'

'You don't want me to drop by? Fine, I'll leave you the fuck alone.' he snarled.

He marched to the door, stopped, and reached for something in his back pocket. He chucked the keys on the cabinet, opened the door and stopped dead as, in front of him, stood Tom.

Chapter Fifteen

Tom's face went to Alan, then to me, and he raised an eyebrow. God, now my brother thought we were sleeping together too, and how did he get inside the block? Did he ring the buzzer and I didn't hear it? Maybe he caught a neighbour coming in on his way. I hadn't planned for them to meet, Alan and my older brother. Alan wasn't a boyfriend so they didn't have to, although at some point they would, given the situation. I rubbed my clammy hands against my pyjama bottoms. Alan cast a backward glance at me.

'Tom,' I said in a voice that sounded more like a squeal than a greeting. I had to ease the awkwardness. Tom's eyes went to Alan.

'Hi, I'm Alan,' he said.

'Oh,' Tom said. 'I'm Tom, Phoebe's brother.'

Alan nodded.

'Is this a bad time?' Tom asked. 'I was in the neighbourhood. I thought I would drop by and check up on you, but I can always get a coffee or something.'

'No need. I was just leaving,' Alan said, walking past Tom. 'Nice to meet you.'

'Yeah, well… same here,' Tom said.

Tom shut the door and I crossed my arms under my chest and looked down at my feet.

'So that is the infamous Alan,' Tom said, his voice reeking with sarcasm.

I didn't have time for this, and I had to process Nash coming back here with more questions. The neighbours hearing me and Adele yelling at each other and Alan lying for me. It was best not to mention any of this to Tom as it would raise more questions.

'Cup of tea?' I said, 'I was about to make one?'

'Sure,' he said.

I went into the kitchen, putting on the kettle, and cleared the mug Alan drunk from earlier.

'What was he doing here, Phoebe?'

'He came to check up on me.'

'Did he? How very nice and thoughtful of him. Are you sleeping with him?'

'Tom!' I gasped.

'I'm sorry, but I have to ask, you are into him after all,' he pointed out. 'All of your issues started when this guy came along.'

I opened the cupboard and took out a fresh mug. 'Adele and I had issues before he came along. It surfaced because… well…'

'Adele started dating him and all hell broke loose,' Tom said. 'Look, you're a beautiful girl, Phoebe.'

I placed the mug in front of him.

'Where are you going with this?'

'I'm saying to be careful. This guy might be playing you both, Adele goes missing, and now I come to visit my baby sister and find him here.'

'I'm not sleeping with him,' I said, ignoring his statement.

Tom sighed.

'Honestly, I'm not. I wouldn't do something like that.'

Tom cast me a suspicious look.

'Tom!' I yelled.

'Okay, Phoebe, I believe you, it's not you that's the problem here but him.'

'You don't know him.'

'And I suppose you do?'

'Can we drop it? I don't want any lectures from you. I know what I'm doing.'

'Do you?'

'Yes, and stop talking to me as if I am an idiot, okay? Now, how are Mum and Dad?'

After a stiff conversation about our parents and his work, Tom walked to the door, his head turned towards the cabinet where Alan's key lay. Tom turned, facing me.

'The guy had keys to this apartment?' he asked.

'Yes, Adele gave them to him, that was why he was here, to hand them over,' I lied.

'Adele was seeing this guy for just three months and gave him keys to this apartment? How daft was she?' Tom asked, unable to hide his incredulity.

'Tom, please, let's not get into this.'

'How about we get into this, Phoebe, I mean let's face it, Adele isn't going to be nominated for the friend of the year any time soon, she treated you like dirt. You should have stopped talking to her the moment she went after the guy you were seeing at the time.'

'She is missing.'

'It changes nothing, just because she's missing it doesn't mean she's a nice person. I never liked her, and I made it pretty clear. You are too forgiving. It's a nice quality to have, but you tolerated her bullshit for long enough.'

'She's missing. She's a victim,' I shouted.

We stared at each other as a frosty silence fell over the room. Tom broke eye contact and puffed out his cheeks.

'I'm your brother, and I'm worried about you.'

'You don't have to worry.'

'I want you to be careful, okay,' he said.

'I know.'

He kissed me on the cheek and his eyes flickered at the keys one more time before he left.

If Nash finds out that Alan lied, he'll be in trouble. I couldn't get it out of my head; why had he lied for me? Me, of all people. Someone he didn't like. Was he doing it for Adele? To be nice to her friend because he felt sorry for me? Was I an object of his pity? Tom was right. Adele wasn't nice to me. When she was nice, it had to benefit her.

I thought about how Alan behaved before he left, and I didn't think it gave him the right to be angry. So, he came and watched over me because I was upset. I didn't need to be rescued; I wasn't looking for a white knight. What did he expect me to do for his effort? Clap my hands like Adele would have done, smother his face with kisses? Why was I comparing myself to Adele? She was missing and I was here.

I slept for most of the day and when I woke up, it was getting dark out. I opened the fridge, there was nothing but a piece of cheese and some lettuce. Not even bread to make a sandwich. I sighed. I'd forgotten about the groceries, but with all that had been going on, it was the last thing on my mind. There was wine, though. I poured myself the yellowish liquid that looked like piss and ordered groceries online. I put music on and paced around the living room with my glass of wine. I sat on the sofa, then on the floor, gave up and went to the window. The lights in Alan's apartment were on. The song that was playing made me feel warm. The keys were still on the cabinet where he had chucked them. I showered and made myself look presentable. I didn't overdo it. I didn't want to give the impression it was for him. It was for me to feel less of a zombie. I came across the now non-working cuckoo clock hanging on the wall, took it off and opened the drawer where I'd hidden the book earlier and collected his keys. It was time to come clean; no use trying to find a way to go in his place to put the book back. I bet he'd noticed it was missing and knew I took it. I put a beige coat over my black outfit and shoved the keys in my pocket. I dumped the clock in the bin and looked at his block. The lights were still on. Someone was coming out and I crossed the street and waved at the woman to leave the door open. I located his door, pulled in my stomach and knocked.

Alan's eyes were cold when he answered the door and said nothing. I jangled the keys like a carrot in front of him.

'They're yours.'

Despite Tom's warnings and suspicions over Alan, I had to find out things about him, why there was no trace of him on the internet and social media. What was going on between him and Adele, was their relationship as passionate as they painted it? To do this, I had to get to know him, find out everything there was to know about this leather jacket-wearing stud with blue eyes. To know why he owned the same copy of the book. It could be just a book where two lovers owned the same copy or it could be there was something more to it than that, the answer to everything.

'Why?' Alan asked.

'I'm sorry. I was being a bitch,' I said.

He blinked at me, then opened the door.

'Yes, you were a bitch,' he said.

The apartment was a bit messier than the last time I had been in it. There were bottles of beer on the coffee table, newspapers with stories about Adele, an empty pizza box, an ashtray with cigarette butts, with bubble gum wrappers beside it. I placed the hardback on the coffee table. Alan stared at me as if I were a lunatic.

'I took it... and Adele had a copy, so I got curious.'

'Are you admitting you stole a book from me?'

'Not stole, borrowed,' I corrected him.

'I wondered where it might have gone.'

So he'd noticed. Of course, he had. Organised people notice when things go missing.

'If you'd asked nicely, I would have let you borrow it,' he said, his voice all warm.

My stomach fluttered and heat rose to my cheeks, making me blush; it was inappropriate to feel this way.

He ran his hand through his greasy hair. 'I was heading out to get a bite to eat. Care to join me?' he asked.

'I would love that.'

Chapter Sixteen

We sat across from each other in a pub, a few blocks away from the apartment. It was quiet and seventies music was playing. The orange light made Alan's face look merry. A pint stood on the table for him, and a glass of white wine for me. We haven't said a word to each other yet, only smiling as if we were two teenagers going on a first date and didn't know what to say or do. Alan was shy and timid; he wasn't normally like this. At least, not around Adele, but she had a talent for making people, or I should say, men, relax in her company. I took a sip of wine. Was he tempting me, luring me deeper into his web and then would swallow me whole? What if I sank so far, I would end up missing, just like Adele? That thought alone made me shiver. Tom's warning came to me. Adele went missing after this guy came along. Was I sitting across from a handsome psychopath? I was over-analysing things. We ordered our food and I learned he was a vegetarian. I didn't know that about him. I ordered fish and chips. What would Adele say if she saw us together in a pub ordering dinner? We were doing nothing wrong. And Adele couldn't see us together. Or could she? I pushed this thought to the back of my mind and thought about what to say to him. There was so much I could talk to him about. Knowing details about him was one of them.

'Did you like the book?' he asked.

'I found it depressing.'

'Really? Why?'

'The ending was sad. She had to kill her brother to save her parents.'

'I thought it was great... I don't read a lot.'

'Why did Adele have a copy?'

'I don't know...' he said. 'She saw it on my bookshelf and ordered one for herself. At least she didn't steal it,' he held my gaze while saying this, and I blushed.

He was flirting with me again or I thought he was. I wouldn't know even if it knocked me on the head.

'Borrow,' I said.

'Yeah, yeah, are you a bookworm or do you just like to steal books?' he teased.

'You're terrible,' I said, covering my face with my hands.

'What's your favourite book?' he asked.

'*The Bell Jar.*'

He nodded. The food arrived and since I hadn't eaten all day, I was ravenous.

'Are you going back to university?' he asked after we began to tuck into our food.

I drizzled some vinegar on my chips. 'Not for now. It's the last thing on my mind.'

'Do you miss her?'

I dipped a chip into the ketchup and popped it into my mouth. It worried me not knowing where Adele was; if she was safe.

'I do.'

Alan walked fast, as if in a hurry. Why would someone be in a rush to go home? He opened the communal door for me, using his key.

'Thank you for tonight. I needed the distraction,' he said leaning closer and giving me a peck on the cheek.

'You're welcome,' I said and watched him walk away.

I went back to the apartment. Adele might have gone missing, but she was everywhere. She was in my apartment, at Alan's. She'd had dinner with us. She lay beside me on the bed.

Dylan came to see me. He had been away in New York for work and apologised for not getting in touch sooner. I poured a glass of wine even though it was too early, but Dylan didn't refuse the offer.

'You don't have any idea where she might have gone?' he asked.

'No, these past few months… when she started dating Alan, she became… distant.'

'But she's your roommate and best friend,' he stated.

'Yes, but that didn't mean she would tell me everything.'

'So, Adele had secrets?'

'Everyone has secrets, Dylan.'

'Do you have secrets, Phoebe?'

What was he getting at?

I gulped my wine. 'No, I'm an open book.'

'Alan told me you had dinner with him yesterday,' Dylan said.

And of course, Alan was going to brag with his friend.

'He's the only person who understands what I'm going through,' I said innocently.

'Of course,' he said. 'And the police haven't given you any updates yet?'

I shook my head. 'Nothing.'

'Where could she have gone off to?' he said, almost to himself.

I stood and walked to the window. Alan's curtains were closed.

'That's what I'm trying to find out,' I said.

'Are you going to look for her?'

'I believe she's out there somewhere. I can't wait for the police.'

'You would be interfering.'

'What are they going to do?'

'Er… arrest you.'

'I always wanted to see myself in a mugshot,' I said.

Dylan laughed and stood.

'Are you going?' I asked.

'Yes, but if you need anything, anything at all, call me, okay?'

I walked Dylan to the door and he gave me a peck on the cheek. All those pecks on the cheek in less than twenty-four hours. There must be something in the air. I went to Adele's room and began my work. I tore out drawers and emptied their contents on the floor. I searched and searched, tearing her room apart. She was so disorganised, Adele had to have left a trail of breadcrumbs to where she had gone. Of course, whatever was there, the police might have taken it, but it didn't hurt to take a second look. What if this was all an act, the mess, but she was an immaculate planner? What if I thought I knew her, but all I knew was that version of her, the bubbly person who got a lot of male attention? What if there was another layer beneath her? I grabbed Adele's copy of Lost and Found and rummaged through the papers, not knowing what I was trying to achieve by doing this. There was nothing. I dumped them and the hardback tore from the cover. I continued to search and groaned when I found nothing then cleared everything away to the best of my ability. I picked the hardback off the floor as I reached for the cover at the back. There was something handwritten there. Passwords. By the looks of it, the police hadn't bothered with the book at all. Why had Adele written the passwords there? Did she hope someone would find them as a clue? Or was it Adele being Adele? Her laptop was in an evidence bag. The passwords were for her Facebook and Gmail accounts. I had to log into her Facebook raising no flags. One of her coat pockets had a hole in the interior. There was something small under there I discovered as I yanked the coat from the hanger and tore the interior with my fingers. A train ticket dated a month ago to Edinburgh was tucked in there. Adele had mentioned nothing to me about going to Edinburgh. I would have remembered if she had. What was in Edinburgh that Adele had to go there without telling me? Adele had secrets, but who didn't? I glanced at the hardback. What was the connection between her and that damn book? Alan had told me she'd ordered a copy when she saw it among his collection of books. Why that book? Adele must have read it then. The theme was like the book, the brother went missing and now Adele had gone missing. I placed the cover of Lost and Found with the passwords, the train ticket, and the book on the kitchen counter. I slid the book towards me. Adele was out there, and not far. Somewhere where she could see me, but I couldn't see her and that chilled me to the bone.

Chapter Seventeen

I was about to open the book when there was a knock on the door. I sighed and went to answer it. It was from Alan.

'I gave you back the key for a reason,' I said.

'I didn't want to barge in on you. I was going to get a drink, want to join?'

'Where?' I asked.

'Somewhere secluded.'

'Alan, where were you the night Adele disappeared?' I asked.

His stare was icy cold.

'Sorry, but I have to ask,' I said.

'I already said I was out that night; the people who were there verified it,' he said.

'And who were those people?'

Another haughty glare. 'A band I was working with, what is this?'

'Okay, sorry I asked,' I said. 'I could use a drink myself. I'll meet you at the place.'

'Fine. Wait for me in the club's corridor.'

'What club?'

'The one we went to with Adele and Dylan. The secret one that locks people in.'

'Of all the places in the city, why there?'

'It's discreet. Meet me in an hour. I'll give you my number. Text me when you get there.'

After I paid the fare for my taxi, I looked at the run-down bar. Nobody would know there was a club hidden underneath. I walked in and heads went up. It smelled of beer and although smoking indoors was now banned, I could still smell it in the air. I kept my head low as I went to the far end and opened the door. I looked to my left and my right. Not a single soul was in there. I sent Alan a text and waited. Five minutes passed and no reply. I tapped my phone against the palm of my hand. My anxiety increased. I heard a door slam and I jumped. My heart thumped against my chest. A figure approached and I sighed with relief when Alan came into view. He glanced at me and swaggered along and I followed him, thinking how seductive he was without being obvious. He was a man who wore his beauty with grace and elegance, unaware of the power he possessed or, he knew but didn't display it. No wonder Adele fell so hard for him. He opened the door and I was enveloped by music. The smell of body odour and perfume danced in the air. The sexual energy was alive as it vibrated through the walls of the club. I'd have preferred we went somewhere tamer to have a drink. What was it about him and this club? How did Alan find out about it? I walked past the dancer who wore leather and fishnets tights. Her face was covered in a mask, like Cat Woman. Was Alan into this kind of scene? Was he into BDSM? Did he and Adele try something kinky?

I thought how careful I had to be here; it was a dangerous game I was playing. I had to be vigilant and alert. Alan went to the bar and ordered drinks. We clicked the bottles of beer. The beer tasted bitter and my mouth was dry and I took more sips. He walked past me. I didn't know if I should follow him or not. He stopped and glanced back at me. White light glowed behind him, then red and blue. Like a sheep, I followed my shepherd. We went into the room with the purple sofas; there were no dancers tonight. A sense of uneasiness came over me. Why did he ask me to join him for this drink and accompany him to this club when any girl would be happy to join him? Was he playing a game with me? I sat down and sipped my beer, wishing he'd got something stronger. He was grieving, however, and he would not ask girls out when his girlfriend was missing. That would make him an arsehole, not to mention what that would look like to the police.

'You okay?' he asked.

I nodded. 'What is this place?'

'It's a club,' he said, making me feel stupid.

'I know it's a club but why's it hidden, how do you know about it?'

'A band did. We used to come here after recording.'

'Is this a sex club?' I asked.

Alan smiled, took a sip from the beer, and cast me a sharp glance. 'More like a fetish club,' he said.

'Aren't they the same thing?' I asked.

Two men walked in and looked at us before sitting down. They were both older and wore black suits and black shirts, no ties. Alan ignored them. I took a sip from my beer.

'It depends on what angle you look at it. I like to come here because it's discreet,' he said.

'So you're interested in the—'

His blue-grey eyes were set on me and my cheeks went red. It was none of my business, yet I was curious.

'Never mind,' I blurted.

'What were you going to ask, Phoebe?'

'How did you—' I stopped halfway, embarrassed.

'Yes?'

'How did you know I was looking?'

He raised an eyebrow. 'Looking? Where?'

'You know where, Alan. That night, you looked directly at me as if you knew.'

My cheeks coloured. Alan took a sip of beer and looked at the two men who had vodkas on their table and were too deep in conversation to pay any attention to us.

'Adele told me.'

'She told you as in you mean it was her idea?' I said incredulously.

'Adele said you had a crush on me.'

'Yes, you told me that and she made fun of me because of it.'

What else did she tell him? Did they laugh at me when they lay in their damp, sex-stained sheets while exchanging post-coital cigarettes? Adele knew nothing about boundaries. You wouldn't share your girlfriend's secrets with a guy you just met, or with anyone. Adele wouldn't expose me or stand between me and a guy ever again.

'She said you used to peek at the window—'

I raised my hand. 'That's enough.'

The two men looked at us. I moved away from Alan and pushed a strand of hair behind my ear.

'All good?' one of the men said.

He was in his late forties and handsome with olive skin and dark luminous eyes.

'All good,' Alan said cheerfully.

The man returned to his drink. Alan rubbed his jaw. This club was weird.

'So, we're locked in here?' I said.

'Not yet, it shuts people in around midnight,' Alan said.

'I'm going to get a drink, you want something?'

'I'm fine,' he said.

I walked past the men's table and felt the heat of their gaze until I left the room. I went to the main room. On the platforms stood women dressed as belly dancers, dancing to an Arabic melody and since we weren't in an Arabic country, I couldn't help but find the scene offensive. I ordered myself a glass of wine and leaned by the bar, watching the dancer swinging her hips. Someone came to my side. It was Alan. He lit a cigarette. The dancer glanced right at us and winked. She wasn't looking at *us*, there was only one person she was looking at. Alan. I rolled my eyes.

'I'm sorry,' he said in my ear.

'It's fine,' I said.

'I am flattered though.'

'Flattered about what?'

'You know.'

The music changed. Steam began to pour into the room and the lasers beamed across, casting pink, green and blue lights. Alan said something, but the music was so loud, I couldn't hear him. Through the dancing bodies, I made out a woman leaning against the wall. Her hair was like mine and she was wearing a replica of my beige coat and round sunglasses. It was me, but it couldn't be me.

Chapter Eighteen

Alan glanced over his shoulder to see what I was looking at. A crowd gathered, covering the woman. When they moved away, she'd vanished. Did I imagine her? Was I losing my mind? She looked like me, but not entirely; something about her was different. I backed away from Alan. I wanted to get out of this place. Heat rushed through my body, into my head, making it buzz, and the room spun. My heart rolled into my rib cage. The faces blended into one, the beat of the music vibrated into my brain almost causing it to explode. I placed my hand on my beating heart as the walls were closing in, making me claustrophobic. I was locked in this club, and the panic surfaced even more. Alan moved away, I crouched down by the wall. Who was that woman? Alan returned a few minutes later, but I couldn't tell. He crouched down in front of me.

'Can you stand?' he asked.

I nodded.

I sat on the sofa in my apartment drinking a glass of cold water. Alan had got us out of the club. He must have thought I was mad. I knew what I'd seen: a woman with her hair like mine, dressed like me. What was going on? Who was that woman? Adele? Someone else? Who? Alan didn't question me and I didn't feel like talking about it. I was still getting my head around it.

I left Adele's bedroom door open and Alan saw the mess I'd left in there. The heap of clothes on the floor, the mountain of shoes and the drawers out of their place, the closet doors wide open.

He looked back at me, aghast.

'I was looking for something,' I said.

'You don't say,' he said.

Alan marched to the kitchen and opened the top cupboard, found a bottle of vodka which I didn't know was there and poured a shot in a glass. Alan had had time to familiarise himself with this apartment, I noted, and this thought didn't comfort me. He came into the living room and sat across from me. I didn't think he'd noticed the book cover with the list of Adele's passwords, and the train ticket on the counter.

'Did you find anything?' he asked after he took a shot of vodka.

I pointed at the counter. He sighed and stood. He inspected the counter, holding the cover.

'I lived here for three years and didn't know we had vodka in there,' I said.

'Adele told me about it, don't worry, Phoebe, I didn't go around looking through drawers and cupboards, if that's what you're worried about,' he said.

My cheeks went red and I took a sip of water.

'Have you tried those yet?' he asked.

I shook my head.

'Why not?'

'I can't just log into her Facebook or email, now can I? The police might track it. He tore the cover, folded it and slid it in the back pocket of his jeans.

'Hey,' I said

He lifted an eyebrow. 'What?'

'You just tore the book cover,' I said.

'Yeah, well… I'll give you my copy, don't worry about it,' He said. 'I'll see what I can do.'

I didn't want him to take the list since I didn't have a photo of it.

'Can you take a photo with your phone? I don't have a copy of the list,' I protested.

'I'll give it back once I'm done, now you need to rest.'

Alan was making coffee the next morning when I woke up. I didn't know if he'd slept on the sofa or gone to his place and come back, but I hadn't heard the door. Did I want this closeness? This felt sudden and it left me overwhelmed and confused. He loved Adele, and now she was gone and I was here. I was the link, a connection to Adele.

'Are you better?' he asked.

'Slightly.'

He leaned against the counter and took a sip of coffee. 'What happened in there?'

'You didn't see her?'

'Who?'

'A woman.'

'They were plenty of women,' he said incredulously.

'She looked like me,' I said.

'She looked like you?'

'I mean, she had her hair like mine, dressed like me.'

'You have a stalker, congratulations,' he said.

'That's not funny.'

He put his hand up. 'Okay, I'm sorry.'

'I think it was Adele.'

He placed the mug down. 'Wait, you're telling me that Adele is disguising herself as you? Why would she do that?'

'I don't know. Did she mention anything to you?'

His face was dark now. 'Oh yes, I forgot to mention that my girlfriend is a psycho and is jealous of you, told me she's going to go missing and dress like you to fuck with your head and told me not to tell anyone.'

'I'm sorry, but I have to ask. I don't know what's what anymore.'

'Phoebe… run yourself a bath and relax.'

'Where are you going?' I asked, alarmed.

'I know someone who can help me with the passwords raising no flags.'

I stared at him dumbstruck. Who? 'And you're suggesting I run myself a bath instead of doing something?'

He went to the door. 'That's exactly what I'm telling you.'

What I could do was speak to Hannah and Janice again.

The stares weighed heavily on me as I stood by the university entrance. I wondered what went on in the students' heads. Did they think I had something to do with Adele going missing? I was the last person who had seen Adele before she disappeared. Adele had gone missing and I had become the centre of everyone's attention. It was lunchtime and I spotted Hannah and Janice sitting on a bench and they nearly choked on their salads when they saw me approach.

They jumped to their feet. 'Oh my God,' both said at the same time as if they'd practised this just in case I showed up.

'How are you? Oh, come here,' Hannah said.

Hannah pulled me to her as if we were best friends. They both spoke at once. Have you heard anything? Did you hear from Adele? Was I coming back?

'Girls, please,' I snapped, 'And no, I have heard nothing as yet, and I'm not coming back, I need more time.' I took a deep breath, 'Did Adele mention to you about going to Edinburgh?'

They looked at each other. 'No,' Hannah said.

'Why would she go there?' Janice asked me.

'That's what I'm trying to find out.'

I turned to leave, then changed my mind.

'Did she buy hair dye when you were together?'

They looked at me strangely. 'Hair dye?' Hannah asked.

Of course, if she'd planned to buy hair dye as part of her plan, Adele would buy it alone, but it didn't hurt to ask. I was convinced that the woman I saw at the club was Adele. It would make sense she would change her look and dye her hair since her photo was all over the papers and someone would recognise her. To go missing, you have to become a ghost. But why look like me, that was what I was trying to get my head around.

'No, she didn't,' Janice said.

'Ta.' I said and walked off.

Chapter Nineteen

I couldn't get the image of that woman in the club out of my mind. I haven't heard a word from Alan and I sent him a text but got no reply. I read the book again and then I got to thinking. Why did Alan suggest the club to have a drink? He said people minded their own business there, yet I saw the woman that very night he invited me. What if he and Adele were in it together to freak me out? That would be twisted and disgusting, but I knew nothing about the guy and he was too clever to reveal details about himself. I had to get to him to talk.

The buzzer went off. Janice stood by the door wearing a look of disapproval upon her face.

'What are you doing?' she asked.

'What?' I asked.

'Going around asking questions.'

'I'm trying to get to the bottom of why Adele disappeared and what might have happened to her,' I said.

'You should leave that to the police.'

'And look at what a good job they're doing,' I said.

'You think Alan took her to Edinburgh?' she asked.

'I don't know. Maybe.'

'How can you not be sure when you're living with her?'

'Adele was spending more time with him than here.'

She lowered her head. 'Okay, fair enough. How are you holding up?'

'I'm stressed.'

She bit her bottom lip. 'You know, because we're Adele's friends, it doesn't mean you're not our friend. We always tried to invite you to join us, but you refused,' she paused, taking a deep breath, 'What I'm trying to say is, you can find a friend in us in these hard times.'

I was touched. 'Thank you, that's very kind of you,' I said.

'Anyway, I'd better be going, don't forget it's good to talk.'

What if that woman would be there tonight? I have never been to the club alone. It made me nervous to go there by myself, but I had to find out what was going on. I took a taxi there and went to the bar, not making eye contact with anyone. I made my way to the corridor and opened the door to the club and the music came alive.

There was a woman who had legs wrapped around a man, and I was sure they were getting it on. I went to the bar and got myself a drink. Eighties music was blasting on the speakers and everyone was dressed in leather and chains. I sipped my drink, scanning the faces. Everyone blended into one. I finished my first drink and ordered another. As I turned away from the bar to face the club, I did a double-take. Alan was walking towards me, puffing on a cigarette. Heat flashed throughout my body; how dare he follow me here? I had to do this alone. If the woman showed up here tonight, what do I do? Confront her? Alan was a distraction I didn't need. I walked towards him as the uneasiness swept over me. Had he followed me here? Or was he here with someone and saw me?

'How did you know I was here?' I demanded.

'I saw you coming out of the apartment.'

'And you followed me here?'

'I'm sorry about this, but this is not a place where a girl comes alone.'

How come that woman was alone then I wanted to ask, but I swallowed the words down.

'What are you doing here, anyway?' he asked.

'I came looking for that woman. Why didn't you reply to my text?'

'I did.'

'No, you didn't.'

'Check your phone, Phoebe, you'll find it there,' he snapped, 'Go on, check.'

I took out my phone and there was a text message. He'd sent it fifteen minutes before I left the apartment.

I'd drop by later X.

I stared at the X.

'Well,' I said.

He looked down at me and the blue lights cast a glow on his face.

'Well, what?' he asked.

'Did you find anything?'

'I did.'

I waited for him to elaborate, but I was faced with a blank wall. It was going to be hard to get to him. He took me by the arm and led me to another room. From his inner pocket, he produced sheets of papers and handed them to me.

'Read them when you're at home,' he said.

'Okay,' I said and placed the printouts in my bag.

'They're Adele's emails, Facebook chats,' he said.

'Thanks. The paper?'

'What paper?'

'Of her passwords.'

He broke eye contact and produced it from his back pocket.

'Any news?'

'No, nothing.'

He rubbed his face. 'Are you sure the woman you saw was Adele?'

'I think so.'

'So, you're not sure?'

'It had to be her.'

'Let me get you a drink,' he suggested. 'Wait for me in the other room like last time.'

I nodded and we parted ways. There were dancers dressed in leather bikinis. I pushed a strand of hair behind my ear and found a secluded spot in the corner. Alan came across clutching two beers and sat beside me and lit a cigarette.

'Can I have one?' I asked.

'I thought you didn't smoke.'

'I don't,' I said and took a cigarette.

Alan looked at his hands. 'I was in a relationship for four years before Adele. There were a few hooks-ups after that but… I needed time… when Adele came along, I was clear with her from the start, I didn't want another relationship but she said, she was looking for a casual hook-up but I don't know… something changed.'

'Adele was after you,' I said.

'You mean she tracked me down?'

'Yes, because of me.'

'I don't get this rivalry between you two and how I got dragged into this.'

'It's not rivalry, it's…' I trailed off, trying to find the right word.

Twisted that what I'd call it. We were friends but something changed, we grew to be different people. Adele the peacock and me the simple girl who wanted to achieve things.

'I don't know what to call it anymore and you dragged yourself into it because you couldn't help yourself,' I said.

He narrowed his eyes at me, cold and piercing. 'Is that what you think?'

'You were out of a relationship, you wanted a rebound and there she was offering herself to you.' I stood up.

'Adele wasn't a rebound.'

'No?'

'There was another girl before Adele. She was the rebound.'

All these women who paraded into his life.

'I see,' I said.

'What do you see?' he asked.

'Have you ever felt trapped,' I asked, changing the subject.

'Trapped?'

'Yes, like you're in a cage and you're too big for it.'

He must have thought I was some sort of freak.

'Yeah, I guess so...' he said meeting my gaze. 'Is that how you feel right now?'

'I feel that way all the time.'

'Tell me something about yourself.'

'What do you want to know?'

'I don't know… anything,' he remarked.

I sighed and stared at the dancer. 'I did nothing stupid or foolish.'

He smirked. 'Like being here with me in this club?'

'You're the one who stalked me over here,' I said.

He smiled. 'I didn't stalk you. I knew what you were up to, and I came to make sure you don't get in any trouble.'

'Worried about my welfare, aren't you?'

'What can I say, I'm a gentleman.'

Chapter Twenty

The curtains were wide open when I got in the apartment, and my body turned to ice. They'd been closed when I left. I had the creeping sensation that someone was in the apartment. First, I thought it was Adele, but now? Was she getting in and out of the apartment? But Adele didn't have the key, the police had found it in her bag and why would she do that? It makes no sense. She could have made a copy and if Adele dyed her hair black, the neighbours wouldn't give her a second glance thinking it was me. My ears prickled with the faint sound of ticking like a clock. My hair stood on end. I slowly turned to where ticking was coming from, shitting my pants.

Tick-Tock.

There it was as if it was never taken out of the apartment and deposited into the bin, the cuckoo clock working just fine. It was nearing midnight and the bird came out, in and out, in and out, and I screamed.

DC Nash was taking the notes, and DS Williams asked the questions.

'So, you're saying you threw it out?' he asked.

'Yes.'

'You didn't think to have the clock checked to see what was wrong with it?' Nash asked.

I crumpled a tissue in my palms. Bits of it were on the floor.

'I didn't want it there,' I said.

'Really, how so?' DS Williams asked.

I couldn't take it anymore. 'Instead of asking me about the bloody clock, why don't you focus on the bigger picture someone came here, opened the curtains and hung the clock on the wall…' I paused.

Alan walked in and both detectives looked at him. I had sent him a panicked text after I called Nash. I should have texted Tom instead of Alan, but I didn't want to worry him and if he told my mum it would be worse. I didn't want to tell them anything, not yet.

'It wasn't the first time I've found the curtains wide open either,' I continued.

Both Nash and Williams turned their attention to me.

'So, you're saying it's not the first time this happened? Why didn't you tell us about it?' Nash asked.

'I wasn't sure.'

'You weren't sure,' she repeated.

Williams was inspecting the front door. 'No sign of a break-in,' he announced.

I wanted to slap him.

'Someone has a key,' I said.

'Someone has your key?' Nash said.

Could she stop repeating my words? I didn't think she believed me. She kept passing suspicious glances at Alan.

'Yes, it could be Adele. Maybe she made a copy of the key to this apartment and left the original in her bag.'

'And why would she do that? Come back here?' Nash asked.

'I don't know. To scare me, perhaps.'

'Your friend goes missing and now someone has a key to your apartment and is coming and going, opening your curtains and putting back the clock you've thrown out,' Williams said as if to make sense of the situation.

'Does someone else have keys apart from you and Adele?' She paused and passed another glance at Alan. 'Boyfriends maybe?'

'I have a copy,' Alan said. 'Adele gave it to me.'

All eyes went on him. 'And you didn't ask for it back?' Nash asked me.

'No,' I said before Alan could speak.

'Why is that, Phoebe?'

'I told him to keep it.'

If she had any uncertainties before about us sleeping together, she sure as hell was convinced now.

'I see,' she said.

'For the record, were you home this evening?' Williams asked Alan.

Alan puffed on his cigarette. 'I got home for an hour than I met Phoebe for a drink.'

Williams nodded with another. 'I see.'

'Do you mind if we take the clock?' Nash asked.

'Yes, you can keep it,' I said.

She nodded at Williams as he produced a set of gloves and took the clock from its place.

'If you feel unsafe, I suggest you stay with someone.' A pause and another look at Alan. 'You trust.' Making an emphasis on *trust*.

'Can I ask you a few questions?' Williams said to Alan after he packed the clock.

'Sure,' Alan said.

As soon as the door closed, Nash turned to me. 'Since it's police business, I have to ask, what is the nature of your relationship with Alan?'

'We're friends,' I blurted.

'Not sleeping with him?'

The question threw me aback and Nash sensed this. 'I'm asking because it's police business. I wouldn't ask otherwise,' she repeated.

'No. I'm not,' I said.

She crossed her legs; her shoes were shined and spotless, as if she had polished them before walking to my door.

'Are you aware Adele was seeing someone else besides Alan?'

Adele was seeing another man? That was absurd, but Adele adored Alan. Who was she seeing?

I blinked. 'No, I wasn't.'

'As her best friend, she sure kept a lot of things from you,' Nash remarked.

'Even best friends keep secrets from each other,' I said, and I wanted to grab the words and shove them back in my mouth, but it was too late. That would imply I was keeping secrets too. Did Alan know Adele was seeing other people?

'What can you tell me about Greg Miller?'

Where did Greg fit in all of this?

'He's a fellow student of ours,' I said.

'Adele didn't tell you anything about her relationship with him?'

Relationship with Greg? My head was spinning. What was Nash on about? Was there a man Adele wasn't fucking? Did Nash have notes of me having sex with him too?

'No!'

Nash sighed.

What had Alan found on her Facebook? I had been consumed with finding the clock back on the wall, I hadn't had time to read the printouts.

'Your best friend Adele started dating this guy, Alan,' Nash said. 'They were getting quite loved up and he has a key to this apartment provided by Adele. The three of you hung out together and sometimes his friend, Dylan used to join you. The night Adele went missing, there was shouting coming from this apartment and you and Alan claimed you were joking. The twice I came here, I found the gentleman in question in this apartment. Now you're telling me you didn't ask him to give you his key back and someone has been coming into the apartment, opening your curtains and hanging the clock you threw away, are we clear on this?'

I blinked at her. Did she think Alan did this?

'Help me out here, Phoebe,' she went on, 'you're very young and when it comes to guys like Alan, they can have a hold on you.'

'Nothing is going on,' I insisted.

'Adele meets this very gorgeous young man and you developed a crush on him and I don't blame you, we all have eyes and Adele is a beautiful young woman, so are you. Having a crush is harmless, but then jealousy gets in the way. Then there is Greg.'

'What are you trying to say, detective? That I had something to do with Adele going missing so I can have Alan all to myself?'

She stood, snapping the notebook shut without elaborating. 'You'll hear from me soon.'

Chapter Twenty-one

I told Alan to go home. I didn't need his protection. I was pissed at what Nash had told me and I was looking at someone to take it out on and there he was, perfect, always ready to offer me support and comfort.

'Leave the key on your way out!' I shouted at him, shutting the bedroom door behind me.

When I woke up the next day, Alan wasn't there. I thought about going back to class. I couldn't sit there and wait until Adele was found, which she wouldn't be because Adele was disguised as me. I couldn't tell this to Nash. She wouldn't believe me. If someone had to find Adele, it was me. Adele wanted me to find her. Was it Adele coming to the apartment? It couldn't be Alan, not when he was with me. Unless he went in before he stalked me to the club, but it seemed unlikely. I went to the kitchen to make myself a cup of coffee and there were his keys with a note written in neat scribble.

Change the fucking locks!

I didn't go by Alan's advice and change the locks, but I stayed cooped up in the apartment with the door locked and bolted. I never heard from Nash. What was she doing? Had they found any fingerprints on the clock? The news about Adele's so co-called disappearance faded into more recent headlines, and hers was old news. I couldn't help but feel that Adele was playing a twisted game with me.

I went through the printouts Alan had given me. The first Facebook chat was with Hannah and Janice, when they had a group chat. I started to read from the top. To once upon a time. They chatted a lot, so it took a while. Mugs of coffee were filled. When I reached the part three months before Adele's disappearance and the time she met Alan, I read with earnest.

There is this guy whose extra salty and I have low blood pressure and need all that salt all over me.

Who speaks like this? Extra salty? Come on! Did Alan read these? That must have him screaming with laughter. Adele was studying English literature, I'd thought she would compose better, more well-written messages. This text was dripping with cheese. But this was Facebook; it wasn't exactly meant to read like Hemmingway.

Hannah: Who's he?

Adele: His name is Alan; he lives right next door.

Janice: And you're going after him?

Adele: Damn right I am.

Hannah: How're you going to do that?

Adele: I know where he hangs out. I have seen him a few times there and I'm going to get him. He's mine.

Janice: You mean you "stalked him"?

Adele: Whatever.

Hannah: Can we come with you? You can't go alone, I mean this guy could be anybody.

Adele: Watch me.

Adele got him and kept the third date rule before "signing the contract". Her words, not mine. After they slept together, Hannah and Janice wanted details and Adele liked to spill the beans. I had to sit and listen while she described the whole Kama Sutra with every guy she was dating. Not dating—sleeping with. Alan was different, had more class unlike the rest of the fucktards she dated. Hannah and Janice wanted to know his size and there were paragraphs long of fruit and vegetable emoji. Adele didn't want to give them details.

Adele: A lady never tells.

Hannah: Since when are you a lady?

Janice: You were never a lady, you slut. Come on, give us a hint, pretty pleeeease.

Adele replied with one emoji not a vegetable or a fruit but a hot dog. Something was different with Alan and she refused to tell. Next, came our chats and again, did Alan read these? Although there was nothing special, it made me uncomfortable. Her group chat with Hannah and Janice would have humoured him, but her chats with me were bland. Was I bland? I noticed Adele used a different language to chat with me, more formal.

I plan to do some ironing tonight, so prepare your shirts and we'll order in pizza xxx

It felt intrusive reading those messages. I knew what we'd talked about, so I skipped them. I came to the next pages and frowned. Chats with Greg. There were lots of them dating back six months or so. Adele and Greg were meeting regularly. I went back to the party he invited me to. How both Adele and Alan were looking at us. But it wasn't us they were looking at, but me. Did Adele tell Alan about her fling with Greg? She couldn't, not when she was seeing both Alan and Greg at the same time according to these chats. Alan must have read those and the detective might have brought it to his attention, asked him questions about it. Why didn't he say anything to me about them? How did Alan feel that Adele was seeing another man behind his back? I scrolled to the recent ones a week before Greg invited me to the party.

Adele: Ask Phoebe to join you and remove the cobwebs from between her legs.

Greg: Why would I do that?

Adele: Maybe she gets over Alan so I don't have to tiptoe around her anymore. She's like a bomb, not my friend.

Greg: That's an issue you have to sort out with her, don't get me involved.

Adele: Can't you do it? You like Phoebe, right? I mean, she's pretty and cute.

Greg: She's pretty, but I feel like I'll be using her and I like Phoebe.

Adele: Oh, come on.

Greg: What if she doesn't want me "to remove the cobwebs" you do have your way with words, Adele.

Adele: I'm sure you can be persuasive, she's only human. And let me know what she's like, I bet she's like a board and hardly makes a sound.

Greg: Bye!

Angry was mild compared to how I felt. My body quivered like an earthquake about to hit. How did I ever consider Adele to be my friend? How could she even call herself a friend to anyone? Friends don't do these things. Adele needed a guide about how friendships work 101. Or friendships for dummies if such a thing existed. Greg, that bastard! How dare he? And I fucked him. I had the impulse to knock on his door and cause a scene. Was he even a suspect? No wonder Nash suspected Alan and me. Nash must think we had something to do with Adele's disappearance but couldn't prove it. Nash did mention *jealousy*. Alan got jealous of her seeing Greg, and I got jealous because of Alan and Greg. What a mess. That meant Nash knew I had sex with Greg. So did Alan. Bloody fantastic. If she read these messages, however, she had an idea of what Adele was like. Even though that didn't mean shit, to her Adele was still a missing girl. A victim. Adele would get all the sympathy.

Chapter Twenty-two

I had a cup of tea in one hand, a glass of whisky in the other. I wanted to be able to laugh, but all I wanted to do was cry my eyes out. Dylan was a gracious host. I didn't tell him about the chats, but he could tell I was upset. I wanted to speak to someone who wasn't Alan even though he was the one that I had to face, but I didn't want to see him. Alan had sent me several texts.

How are you?

Can we talk?

Hello?

Phoebe?

I don't like being ignored.

What's the matter with you?

I poured a bit of whisky in my teacup and pulled a face as I sipped. My phone came alive casting a glow and Alan's name appeared and I stabbed the phone so hard with my finger, I thought the screen would crack. Dylan had a look of pure amusement and worry.

'Would you like to spend the night?' he asked.

'Spend the night?'

'I can take the sofa. You can take the bed,' Dylan suggested.

'No, it's fine I just need… company,' I said.

'You're under a lot of stress, aren't there any updates?'

His phone went off, making me jump.

'Yeah…' he said to the caller, casting a look at me, 'she's right here. Okay, no worries, mate.'

It had to be Alan. Dylan hung up and placed the phone on the coffee table.

'Alan is looking for you. He sounded worried. He's on his way up here.'

How did he know I was here? I placed the cup of tea and whisky on the coffee table and gathered my things.

'Where are you going?' Dylan asked.

'Out of here.'

'Why?'

'I don't want to talk to him,' I said.

'If you'd told me, I would have told him you weren't here.'

'It's not your fault.'

'I see.'

I looked at him. 'What do you see?'

'You're upset because of him.'

'No, I'm not.'

'Okay, Phoebe, it's none of my business but I'm going to ask anyway, are you sleeping with him?'

'Why does everyone think I'm sleeping with him?'

'Alan is a great guy, and I noticed how you sometimes looked at him. Your friend who is also his girlfriend went missing, you're both going through the same thing, both of you are stressed so it's understandable, I guess.'

'No, it's not understandable and nothing is happening.'

'Okay.'

There was a knock on the door and, for a moment, I considered going through the window just to avoid Alan. Dylan opened the door and they exchanged a few words before I headed past them. I realised I was wearing my coat inside out.

'I'll let you sort out your... difficulties,' Dylan said.

'Thanks,' Alan said.

I didn't bother to stop and turn the coat around. Alan caught up with me and pulled me against the wall.

'What the hell is the matter with you?' he hissed.

'Nothing is wrong,' I said.

'Really? Then what's with the attitude? And fix your coat you look ridiculous,' he snapped.

'How did you know I was here? Do you have a tracking device or something?'

'I took a guess, why are you not answering my calls?'

'I don't want to talk to you.'

'Why? What have I done now?'

'You've done nothing.'

'Look, you're scared, but I'm not the bad guy here. I want Adele to come back as much as you do.'

'Alan, I want her to be found, but her and I are done!'

'What's wrong?'

'I have read the fucking chats, that's what's wrong. I found out about her and Greg, which I am sure you did as well. And about me and… him.'

Alan didn't look too upset about it. If he were, he didn't show it. 'Yeah, I did.'

'Why didn't you tell me when we were in the club?' I asked.

'I thought it was better to see for yourself rather than hearing it from me,' he said and stormed past me.

I followed him, removing my coat. 'So, you had no idea?'

'I'm telling you I didn't. Why do you keep it rubbing it in my face? Stop being so insensitive. Do you think I would have kept on seeing Adele if I knew she was fucking someone else?' he said, his voice breaking.

Men are such selfish jerks. They went off, shagged whoever they pleased while seeing someone, but since they are men, they were excused. But if a woman did it, they'd get all uptight because women weren't supposed to behave that way.

'I don't know, I mean... it's not like I know you that well.'

He took a step towards me. 'I didn't. Stop asking. I curse the moment you crazy bitches came into my life!'

'How am I a crazy bitch? I don't know what I have done to you to cause this kind of contempt,' I snapped. 'And in Adele's defence, she wouldn't have minded if you were fucking someone else. Stop being so judgemental and uptight, I didn't take you for a prude... considering...' I trailed off.

'Considering what!'

'Fuck off, Alan.'

'I will after you tell me if you knew she was seeing Greg?'

I put on my coat, 'No, Nash told me so you can imagine my surprise. Adele's vagina should be London's main attraction. Always open. Always ready.'

Alan stared at me as if it was him I just jabbed. I tried to put on my coat but my hand got stuck. All I wanted was this nightmare to end, to go to sleep and wake up when it was over or not wake up at all.

I went to the apartment and the curtains were closed as I'd left them, but I still checked every room to make sure everything looked fine. I wanted to go and confront Greg about his fling with Adele. I was so angry.. Maybe it was him she went to see the night she disappeared. I texted Janice. We agreed to meet in a café near university during lunch.

Hannah was with her. Janice looked rather worn out and tired, and Hannah looked worried.

'We figured you want to meet us to talk about Adele and Greg,' Hannah said.

'That's exactly what I wanted to talk to you about,' I said.

Did Janice know about this? Why didn't she tell me?

'We told the police we didn't know. We had no idea. We are hurt that Adele didn't tell us,' Janice said.

'You had no idea? You never saw them talk?'

'They talked, yes, but we didn't think they had a fling… I mean…' Hannah said and stopped.

'You mean?'

'You had sex with him,' Hannah reasoned.

I clutched my hand around my coffee cup. 'How do you know?' I asked.

'Adele told us.'

'She told you I had sex with Greg? What else did she tell you about me?'

Hannah and Janice looked at each other. 'That was it, I promise.'

'She did say you had a crush on Alan,' Janice pointed out.

Hannah stared at her as if she'd broken a code.

'It's through me she noticed him,' I said.

'So, you're telling us Adele went after Alan because she knew you had a crush on him, so what?' Hannah asked.

'Admit it, Hannah,' Janice said. 'That's not a very nice thing to do. How would you feel if I did that to you?'

Hannah waved her hand as if dismissing her.

'Did Alan know about Greg?' I asked.

Because Alan said he didn't know it didn't mean I believed him.

'I don't know,' Janice said.

'We know nothing about Alan. We tried to tell her about this, but she got all cross and told us to shut up. Adele didn't speak to us for days because of that. Adele was secretive when it came to Alan. Didn't tell us anything. I mean, what did she know about the guy except he's super-hot?' Hannah said.

'He's off the charts hot,' Janice agreed.

'He doesn't even have Facebook. Who doesn't have Facebook?' Hannah said.

'There are many people who aren't on Facebook,' I argued.

'Yes, those who are hiding under a rock,' Janice said.

'What if Alan found out about Adele and Greg and did something? Like a crime of passion and shit,' Hannah said.

'Girls, back to Greg. Was he questioned by the police?' I asked.

'We heard he was taken to the station several times,' Hannah said, then leaned in closer and I did the same. 'Rumour has it, he's a suspect. He hasn't shown his face around here for days.'

How come there wasn't anything in the newspapers? But Greg has nothing to do with Adele's disappearance because she was pretending she was missing. Or was she? Then who was the woman I saw at the club dressed up as me?

I went down the steps to the tube. Behind me were two girls. One of them was talking about a date she was going on that evening. I took out my phone and texted Janice.

Why didn't you tell me that Greg had been questioned by the police when you came to see me?

A reply came right away.

I forgot.

How can someone forget such an important detail? I sighed. A man in a suit overtook me and nearly hit me with his briefcase to chase after the train. The man squeezed through the closing doors. There was the squeal of metal against metal as the train moved along. Another text came in, it was Alan. I sighed, this felt overwhelming and wrong. I opened the text. It only had three words that sank me deeper into this nightmare.

Dylan is dead.

Chapter Twenty-three

I stared at the text as if the words would somehow be different. It was like a snake crawled into my veins and spread its venom on my entire body, making me nauseous. How could he be dead? No, it couldn't be. How could he be dead when I was at his place the previous night? I went to Google and the headlines jumped at me.

Young Man Found Dead.

Young Man Murdered in his Home.

I covered my mouth with my hands, *murdered*. How? Who killed him? Wasn't Alan with him after I left? My blood went icy cold. Why would someone want Dylan dead? I tried calling Alan, but the call went straight to voicemail. I rushed to Alan's apartment and rang the buzzer, but no one answered. My finger pressed on the buzzer, unable to let it go. A woman carrying groceries climbed the steps. She gave me a strange look before unlocking the door.

I banged on the door. No answer. Maybe he wasn't home? Then where was he? Did he—no, don't think about it. Alan wouldn't do something like this. Would he? Adele went missing and now Dylan was dead. With a shaking hand, I tried the knob and the door opened. My heart stopped, fearing the worst. What if something had happened to Alan too? I felt like an intruder going into his apartment, but did I have another choice? The curtains were shut, making the place look gloomy and from what I could tell it was trashed as if a pack of lions were let loose and destroyed it. Glass was shattered on the floor, books torn off the shelves and scattered on the floor. I took a step forward and the glass crunched under my shoes. Alan was on the sofa, a blanket wrapped around him, staring into space. His eyes were red from crying. I sat beside him.

'Alan…' I said.

What could I say? I'm sorry? I'm sorry for your loss? These were the words he was avoiding. I let him take his time.

'After you left,' Alan began with a small, low voice. 'I went back to his apartment… I stayed about an hour then left… I should have known.'

'How could you have known?'

Alan looked at me square on the face. 'He was stabbed.'

'Jesus.'

'I don't know who would do something like this.'

'First Adele and now this… terrible things happen to the people I care about.'

'Don't talk about that right now.'

'Stay with me,' he said, placing his hand on mine. 'Please…'

'I'm not going anywhere, try to get some rest.'

As he slept, I tried to sort out the mess he'd made. Collecting the books that survived I placed them back on the shelf and put aside the ones that were beyond repair. The copy of *Lost and Found* was destroyed. Most of the pages were torn from the binding, and the cover was ripped into pieces. As I picked up the rest of the books, I came across two cuttings from old newspapers lying on the floor near the sofa. I looked at Alan, who was still asleep, his chest rising and falling. I picked up the first; it was a review of a performance, written by Perry White.

Is this Classical Music? Or Someone in the Wrong Business?

By just reading the headline, I knew this is going to be a five-hundred-word rant. I scanned the words. *Not a talented pianist. Belongs in a rock band, not behind the piano.* By the looks of this journalist, he couldn't stand the musician in question.

The lad looks fed up behind the piano like the doesn't want to be there. My opinion of this bloke and I refuse to call him a pianist remains the same. Allan Styles began playing the piano at the age of seven, the youngest son of the tennis player Martha Styles, the force behind her son's success. Allan went on studying at the prestigious "Royal Academy of Music" yet despite his impressive background, he looks like a minion that is in desperate need of a proper haircut. No charisma, no technique. Another privileged child whose "career" is bought not because of the talent itself.

Allan Styles. Alan Wiley. Was this piece about him? I glanced over my shoulder; Alan was in deep slumber. It had to be about him. Why would he have a cutting from an old newspaper if it wasn't related to him or about him? Alan had changed his name. So that was why I couldn't find anything about him. Why had he changed his name? To start afresh? I went to the next article.

Music Journalist and Critic Found Dead in his Home.

Music critic and journalist Perry White aged 45 was found dead in his home by the maid. White was found tied up, naked, with a leather belt around his neck, strangled to death. Sources say White was no stranger to frequenting fetish and sex clubs and a regular taker of drugs.

There were no witnesses. The neighbours heard nothing suspicious. It's been ruled as a sex game gone wrong.

I took out my phone from my pocket and took pictures of the cuttings with trembling hands. There was also a photograph of a woman holding a baby. She had long auburn hair. I assumed it was a photograph of Alan as a baby with his mum. Alan Wiley. Allan Styles. My head buzzed with this discovery. I went to the window to look at my apartment. I saw myself, the girl who used to gaze out with such longing and wonder at his window. Now she was across the street in that same apartment. Life worked in mysterious ways. I made a cup of coffee and tried to collect my thoughts. There was a dead journalist who despised Alan, believing he made it as a pianist because of the connections his parents had. I never understood this kind of hatred towards the children of powerful, rich parents. Yes, it was easier with parents who had connections, but a minor talent had to be involved, right? Nobody makes it into the music business without being talented, same goes for other careers, such as acting and modelling. I guess the hate towards these children born to privilege involved more that they didn't have to work as hard as the people who came from nothing. At least that was what people spreading this venom assumed.

Adele went missing, and Dylan was murdered. Alan said he was with Dylan. There was a lot of mystery surrounding this guy and lots seemed to go wrong around him. Was I missing something? Alan was still asleep. I went through my phone and ran a few searches. I started with Allan Styles. There had to be more articles about him. Why the particular cutting? The unpleasant one? Why not an article that had nicer things to say? I got a few results from old articles, nothing recent. The last one dated two years ago. I clicked on the first one. A picture came up and it was Alan. No greased hairstyle and quiff, no leather jacket either. Alan must have taken Perry White's remark and got a cool haircut and a whole makeover. Not that he needed it. He was just as stunning in this picture with those piercing blue-grey eyes gazing into the camera and chiselled features. He could have been a model.

'I found you,' I whispered to the old Alan in the picture.

The article was a review of this technically wonderful pianist. There was nothing much, reviews of performances, a few articles and announcements. In one article Alan was described as an upcoming virtuoso. Despite White's nasty remarks, Alan was indeed talented. You have to be, to be described as a virtuoso. So what the hell happened? What could have gone wrong? Alan didn't give interviews. There were three other rants from this

Perry White spreading his hate. I Googled him next, Perry was a puffy faced slight over weight man with thick round glasses. His biography said he was trained to be a musician but remained a journalist. A picture formed; I knew the types like White. A spiteful man who most likely failed to make it as a musician and was jealous of those who were better than he was. Of course, Alan would be a target. He was a young, upcoming, good-looking musician with a bright future. Whose mum was the tennis player. It seemed Perry liked to bully musicians. He shared a special hatred for pianists. There were a lot of articles about his death. Maybe someone did something about the abuse he spread through the media. Terrible, I know. I Googled Alan's mother next, Martha Styles, and this was where I got the most hits. I could see where Alan got his stunning looks from. She had auburn hair with piercing blue eyes and a set of cheekbones so high they'd cut through diamonds. She could have been a supermodel in her younger days. She was the same woman from the photograph cradling a baby in her arms. Martha had quite a career and won many tournaments before marrying her coach and had a baby a year after. Martha returned to tennis but eventually quit to spend more time with her son. She would have two more children. Stephen the eldest, John, and Alan, who was the youngest. Alan didn't talk about his family; it was strange to know he was a son and a brother. It was a silly thought, of course, he had a family, Alan didn't drop from the sky straight into our neighbourhood. I had found Alan and he didn't know it. I googled him again, this time using Alan Wiley and still nothing. I went back to my phone, transferred the two photos into my Dropbox and deleted them off my phone.

What if it was Alan who wrote the book using the pseudonym of Robert Freeman?

Chapter Twenty-four

I didn't question Alan about the cuttings. I didn't want to appear as if I had been snooping. I wasn't; I didn't open drawers and cupboards, they were there on the floor. Alan should have thought about that before he tore the place apart. Alan must have known I had seen them but he didn't question me about it. What if he'd wanted me to see them?

'Can you stay for a few days?' he asked.

His eyes were glassy as if he was about to cry. 'You're the only one I have left.'

The irony. What happened to the sex appeal of a dead slug? He needed that slug now. This was an opportunity for me to discover more about him. Tom called and I locked myself in the bathroom so Alan wouldn't listen to the conversation.

'Where are you?' he asked. 'I dropped by the other day and you weren't there.'

'I'm not in my apartment.'

'I figured so. Where are you? And why are you whispering?'

'I'm at Alan's.'

The silence was so defined, I thought the line went dead.

'Tom, are you there?'

'I'm here.'

'I know you don't approve.'

Who cared what my brother thought? Yes, he had warned me, and yes, there was a lot of mystery surrounding Alan and his past.

'You read in the papers about the guy who was stabbed in his apartment, Dylan?' I asked.

'Yes.'

'He was Alan's friend.'

'Jesus.'

'Alan's gutted so I'm staying with him for a few days.'

'So, his girlfriend goes missing and now his friend is murdered?' Tom questioned, unable to hide his scepticism. 'Phoebe, you are getting sucked into a dangerous game. It's my job to tell you things you don't want to hear. Get out of there. It's none of your business. It has nothing to do with you.'

'Tom, please.'

'YOU DON'T KNOW HIM!' he shouted.

'It's just that Alan was there for me when Adele disappeared.'

'Well, I hope you don't end up missing as well,' he said darkly.

The buzzer went off.

'Phoebe!' Alan yelled.

'Coming!' I shouted. 'I have to go.'

'Phoebe—'

I ended the call before I could listen to Tom. I opened the bathroom door and Nash and Williams were standing by the front door. They gave me a strange look. They wanted to ask Alan a few more questions.

'I already answered all of your questions,' Alan said, unable to hide his irritation.

'I have some errands to run,' I announced.

'Hold on, we have a few more questions for you too,' Nash said in the tone of a teacher who wouldn't let me go to the toilet.

'Oh,' I said.

I sat down next to Alan and they stared at us. How must we have looked under the microscopic eyes of these detectives?

'Where you were the night Dylan was killed?' Nash asked.

Alan stared at them, annoyed, 'I went by Dylan's apartment around eight pm.'

'That's because Phoebe was there,' Williams said.

'Yes, but she went and I stayed for an hour and left,' Alan replied.

'Where did you go after you left Dylan's place?' Nash asked me.

'I went home,' I said.

'Is there anyone who can verify that?' Williams asked.

'I called my mum as soon as I got there, you can verify that with her if you like.'

'We will. Thank you,' Nash said.

'Any news about Adele?' Alan asked.

'That's what we'd like to talk to you about,' Nash said, looking at me.

I waited.

'We found Adele's phone in Hackney. Did Adele know anyone in that area?' Nash went on.

Hackney? Why would Adele go there? Why there, of all places?

'No,' I said.

'Are you sure?' Williams said.

'Yes, I am.'

'What about you?' Nash asked, turning to Alan. 'Did Adele say anything to you about going there or knowing someone in the area?'

'No,' Alan said.

'We ran a fingerprint check on the clock but we could trace nothing,' Williams said.

As I thought.

'Did you notice anything strange about Dylan's behaviour before you left?' Williams asked.

'No,' Alan said.

'What about you?' he asked me.

'No,' I said.

We sounded like tape recorders. Nash and Williams exchanged looks, irritated by the case. They had a missing girlfriend and now a dead friend.. They left shortly afterwards.

Alan went to sit in front of the TV, flipping channel after channel, giving the TV a headache. When nothing seemed to interest him, he stood and collected the music sheets off the floor and placed them back on the piano then sat there staring at the keys.

When the music filled the apartment, I had to stop what I was doing, which was washing the plates, and listen. No wonder he was described as an upcoming virtuoso. I creamed my pants by just listening. Magical was the word to describe it. Why didn't Alan play anymore? What happened? I had to act as if I didn't know any of this. I moved to the sofa, sat down and watched him play. When he finished playing the piece, Alan went on staring at the keys as if they could give an answer or meaning to all of this.

'That was... wow,' I said.

He looked at me. 'I'm not that good.'

Not that good. Now he was being modest, and I liked that about him. 'What was the piece?'

'It's called Gnossienne no. 4,' he said.

'It's lovely.'

'My mum wanted all of us, my brothers and I, to have musical backgrounds. We all do. I'm the youngest. The piano was it for me, started very young, fell in love with music and decided that's what I wanted to do. My mum didn't object, my Dad was a little sceptical.'

'So, you played the piano professionally,' I said stupidly, as if I had no idea.

'Yes, I played professionally for a few years, but I don't enjoy touring, giving interviews that sort of thing. I developed a skill in producing music instead.'

'That's a shame,' I said.

He stood and walked over to me and lit a cigarette. 'Why?'

'You're asking me why, maestro?'

He smiled and sat beside me.

'I have to go back to the apartment.'

'I know. It's selfish of me to keep you here.'

'No, it's not... you've just lost a friend.'

Alan placed his hands on mine. He had beautiful hands. They weren't rough but soft, hands that weren't accustomed to hard labour but those of an artist.

'You too have lost a friend,' he said. 'We are both grieving.'

My eyes went up to his face and he leaned in closer. His lips were wet against mine, soft and tempting. Alan held me to him as if his life depended on it. Our tongues danced and he felt so good, so right. I was melting away, but I had to keep my wits about me. This was all for the wrong reasons. I knew why Alan was doing this, not because he liked me, or wanted me, but to forget, even for a few minutes, a relief to his stress and grief. Somewhere along the way, the idea of him got tainted. Alan was Adele's boyfriend and she was missing. He lay me down on the sofa and unbuttoned my jeans. I would remain the one with the sex appeal of a dead slug, I will always be the slug, slimy and disgusting. The unwelcome guest. The uninvited but I was there, the convenient friend of his girlfriend, that was why he had his hand sliding inside my underwear as if he were prospecting for gold. God. His touch made my whole body vibrate. Alan would end up regretting it, he would blurt "I'm sorry." The unsexiest word in the whole dictionary and move on and I would remain with the feel of him and his I'm sorry. It was the last thing I wanted. I wanted to serve a meaning, a purpose. I wasn't Adele, still, I was her as I throbbed and ached for him but I pulled away jumping up from the sofa. Alan looked at me, hurt. The rejection sweeping in.

'Alan, you're in pain and you're looking for something to forget,' I said. 'I can't give you what you're looking for.'

His eyes narrowed at the floor. Alan looked so young and innocent now. He also looked as if he was about to cry and I wanted to take it all away.

'I can't take it anymore,' he cried.

'If I could, I'd take that pain away.'

'Then come here,' he pleaded.

'That will only make you feel better for a while.'

'So what? At least I would feel something,' he said raising his voice, getting angry realising he wasn't getting what he wanted. I couldn't understand what I could have done wrong. How was this my fault?

'As if you didn't think of me doing that to you,' he snarled.

The rejection had sunk in now.

'That's not the point…' I sighed.

'You're telling me you haven't thought of me fucking you? You're a liar, come on, tell me how did you picture it? You can give me that, at least.'

Alan was unreasonable now. I was his enemy. The cause of his suffering. I wanted to find that pain and kill it.

'Come on, Phoebe, what was it? Or do you just like to watch?'

Shaking my head with disbelief, I reached for my bag and coat. As I opened the door, a woman stood there about to knock. She had auburn hair and blue eyes. There was a look of surprise on her face.

'Oh!' she said.

It was Alan's mum.

Chapter Twenty-five

'Is this a bad time?' Martha asked.

She must have sensed the toxic atmosphere between us. Her eyes passed to me once more, wondering who I was. Her son had a girlfriend who was missing and a friend who was murdered yet he had a girl in his apartment.

'No, this is Phoebe,' Alan said.

She gave me a look of recognition even though I'd never met her before. Alan must have told her about me.

'You're Adele's friend,' Martha said.

Martha was a sophisticated woman with a dainty quality about her. She wore a white coat and smart black trousers and high heels and Chanel No.5 wafted in the air. Her hair looked like it was fresh from the stylist with dark blonde highlights. A Michael Kors handbag was slung over her elegant shoulder.

Had Adele met Alan's parents? Or maybe he had told his mum he was seeing Adele. But how did Martha know about me I wanted to know.

'Yes, nice to meet you. I'm sorry but I have to go,' I said.

'Wait,' she said to me in a tone that made me feel like I was five years old.

'Mum…'

'Don't mum me, young man, why haven't you answered any of my calls? Your dad and I are worried sick!'

'As you can see, I'm grieving.' Alan said.

'Yes, and you grieve surrounded by your family who loves you.'

I didn't have to be there and listen to this. It was too personal, and I didn't want to get involved in any family drama.

Alan rolled his eyes. 'I like it better here and as you can see Phoebe has been rather... attentive.'

His mama bear glanced at me with her eyebrows raised. I stood there with no ability to talk. What did she make of this?

'I understand you're going through a tough time, but being locked in here won't help. I came here to take you back home where you belong,' Martha said, turning back to him.

'I don't want to go back home,' he argued. 'I'm twenty-five years old, not a child. Stop telling me what to do.'

She exhaled. He must have been difficult as a little boy, crying, spoiled even.

'I have to go,' I announced.

'You stay,' Alan said, as if I were a dog, and I wanted to grab something and throw it at him.

His mum glanced at me apologetically, but I still didn't like how her eyes followed every inch of me as if she was forming an opinion of me. Analysing me through my clothes, judging if I was good enough. I wondered what she'd thought of Adele if she'd met her. She would have hated Adele. In her eyes, Adele would be nothing more than a tart.

'Tomorrow a car is coming to pick you up and you'd better be ready,' Martha said in a stern tone.

'Fine. I come under one condition,' Alan said.

'And what that might be?' she said crossing her arms.

There was a pink diamond ring, alongside her wedding ring. An engagement ring, I supposed.

A lot of pros ran in the family, pro coaches, tennis players, and pro pianists and musicians. High achievers with gold stars plastered all over their foreheads.

'Phoebe would come with me too,' Alan said.

Me going with him to his parents' house. Was he nuts? I wasn't family. It was so selfish of him to do this to me; I had a life. I had to find out more about Greg and Adele, and their relationship. I couldn't put everything on hold for Alan. Yes, he was in pain, but that didn't excuse the fact he was being a total ass. I was going through something traumatic too, someone was trying to fuck with my head. Adele was missing, disguised as me, or someone was. Adele wanted Greg to seduce me, she might have broken into my apartment to mess with me, but nobody cared about that because Alan was a top priority. Martha glanced at me once more. Her look was intrusive. She too joined Nash in the *were they, weren't they?*

'If that what it takes for you to come home, then so be it.'

Me, a guest at his mother's house. His mother wasn't going to take me by the arm and lead me to the kitchen and offer to make tea while she got to know me. I would get sympathy points since I was a friend of the missing girlfriend. That was all I'd ever be. How did she know who I was, damn it! Martha wasn't going to deal with me right there and then, but she would. I bet she had questions and, like the police, Martha very much wanted to know what the nature of my relationship with her son was.

I felt drained and exhausted. I was going to Alan's parents' house. Adele would be envious unless, she'd already been, but I didn't think Alan was the kind of guy who would bring home the first girl he met. Not after he had just come out of a four-year relationship. He seemed cautious and sensible. Then why me? Maybe his mum had heard of me from the papers. Or he'd told her about me, but why would a guy like Alan talk about me with his mum? Why did he want me there, I also wanted to know.

It was clear what we were. I was the mouse. He was the cat. And his parents were going to have a mouse in their house. For how long was I expected to stay?

The next morning, I fussed with the packing. All I had packed was a uniform of black turtlenecks and a pair of jeans. Then I removed everything and reconsidered. I sighed, sat on the bed, then went to the kitchen and poured myself a strong cup of coffee. I went to the window; Alan's curtains were closed. Where did his parents live, anyway? I sipped my coffee by the window. The streets were damp from the rain that had poured earlier. Cars rumbled by and a woman with a red coat walked past, nearly slipped, and her handbag dropped on the ground. She picked up her bag then looked around before stomping off. In the corner by Alan's block of apartments was a woman in a beige coat like my own. Long black hair and round sunglasses. The coffee caught in my throat and coughed. I placed the mug down, my heart jolted out of my chest. I reached for my keys and bolted out of the door. I rushed through the corridor to the lift. I wasn't thinking, only acting on impulse, but by the time I was outside, she was gone.

I didn't plan to tell Alan about what I'd seen. I repacked my turtlenecks and jeans then checked the window again, but no one was there. A man in a black coat walked past, talking on his phone. Everything looked normal. Was that Adele or someone involved with her disappearance? Maybe she had disappeared and was held captive or worse while I was going to accompany her boyfriend to his parents' house.

Alan and I came out of our apartments at the same time. His hair must have had two tubes of gel and a can of hairspray. A spotless black car stood waiting by the pavement. I crossed the road to him and he produced a pair of sunglasses from his pocket.

'Why do you want me to come with you?' I said.

'Good afternoon to you too,' he said.

'Answer me.'

'Look, my relationship with my family is good but they like to butt into my life as most parents do and I want no part in what they have,' he said and got in the car.

That didn't explain why he wanted me there. I stood on the pavement looking at where the woman had stood that morning. The window rolled down and Alan's face appeared.

'It's quite a drive, are you getting in or what?'

Chapter Twenty-six

It wasn't a house but a mansion. The country house stood proudly while its sheer size dwarfed me. It was a red-brick mansion with French windows, nine thousand square feet of it. By looking at Alan's statuesque mother, I'd assumed she was rich, but I'd had no idea how wealthy. If Adele were here, she'd be squealing with pleasure, literally jumping up and down, clapping her hands with joy, her eyes with dollar signs in them. It would be like hitting the jackpot. Not only was Alan drop-dead gorgeous, but born into money. A dream come true. Alan came beside me and had a look of indifference on his face. He was raised here. He was privileged. Lucky. I wondered what it must have been like growing up in Surrey, surrounded by all that wealth.

'You grew up here?' I couldn't help but gasp. Who wouldn't?

'No.'

'No?'

'This house was passed on through generations from my mother's side, its old money really. I was raised in Hammersmith before my parents moved to Kensington. Then Mum sold that place and moved here, permanently.'

Would his brothers be here too? It was an intimate family affair and I had no business being involved.

'Why did you ask me to come here with you?'

He narrowed his eyes at me. 'Because I want you here with me, I can't possibly go through it alone.'

'But they are your family,' I reasoned.

'Which can be a little crazy,' he said, walking up the steps of the house.

Alan stopped and turned. 'Are you coming or going to linger outside all day?'

I followed him and he opened the door.

'Mum!' he yelled.

It was like I'd stepped into a gothic novel. The foyer had wooden floors with a dominating staircase. Alan went to the next room. They must have maids and a butler.

'Alan, darling,' his mum called out.

I peeked from the foyer. There were two large rooms with grey sofas and a fireplace, and artwork hanging on the walls. His mum put her arm around her son and cast me a glance. I spotted a fine grand piano in there. Of course, there would be a piano.

'Phoebe,' Martha said cheerfully. 'So thrilled you could join us. Welcome.'

She kissed me on both cheeks and escorted me into the living room while my brain was aching about how much this house might cost. From the windows, I made out a pool and was that a tennis court?

'Thank you for being there for him, it means a lot. This is difficult for both of you. You must be exhausted? Let me show you to your room. My son and I have a lot to discuss. You can freshen up and join us for tea, let's say about…' Martha paused checking her wrist. No watch was on there. 'Three o'clock?'

She couldn't wait to get rid of me, but I was the rodent in her house.

'I can show her to the guest room, Mum,' Alan said.

'It's okay, honey, you relax. You've been through enough already,' Martha said, as if Alan showing me into my room was hard work.

She ushered me out of the room with her hand under my arm and I was so confused.

'I'm very sorry you have to go to this trouble after what you're going through, this must be the last thing on your mind.'

'It's no trouble, really,' I lied.

'Did the police give you more updates about Adele?'

I shook my head.

'Alan told me you and Adele were childhood friends?'

'We were, have you met Adele?'

She gazed at me. 'Why would I meet Adele?'

I blinked at her rapidly. So Adele never met his mum.

'I'm sorry, I thought you must have met.'

'No, dear, Alan told me they had a brief fling. Pretty girl,' Martha said. 'But then again, you all are.'

There was a slight acidity in her voice, as if she'd tasted something bitter. It was clear from the pictures she had seen of Adele that Martha didn't like what she saw. It was like Martha was saying yes, *my son has grown up to be a babe and you bitches all want a piece of him.* The protection of a mother, the lioness protecting her cub, even if that cub was a grown man.

'Staying here will do you good, it will get your mind off things,' she said.

Martha led me up the stairs and the house was stressing me out. All this richness, the hard-oak furniture, the wooden walls, the dark drapes and the wood creaking under me as I walked.

'Did you tell your parents you're here?' she asked.

'Yes.'

'Good,' she said. 'I don't want any trouble with your parents.'

Why would there be any trouble? My mum was against it when I called to inform her I was going to stay with Alan's parents for a few days. Her confusion and dismay were defining. Why on earth would I want to do that?

There were a lot of doors. I wondered if there were any forbidden rooms. We passed a painting of a man who stared disapprovingly at me. Were those people in the portraits distant relatives?

Martha opened an oak door. 'I hope this will be to your satisfaction.'

The room was shabby chic meets Jane Austen novel.

'It's lovely. Thank you.'

Martha nodded and closed the door as if she was banishing me into the room. I lay down on the bed that felt like a dream, but I wished I could die.

I couldn't die though. I stayed on the bed with my hands clasped on my stomach, staring at the striped wallpaper. It was like the house was going to swallow me. I couldn't hear any voices, as if all the sounds in the house were muted out. I got up from the bed and went into the bathroom. There was a large bath, no shower. I kept myself occupied by unpacking, not that there was a lot to unpack. After that was done, I gazed out of the window. It gave me a view of the back of the house. There was a pool. At the far side was a small shed. It looked brand new, or it was never used. It wasn't small like any ordinary tool shed, but much bigger. I turned away from the window, switched on my phone, and browsed the headlines that became the soundtrack of my life. I watched a clip of a blonde reporter standing outside Dylan's apartment talking about the murder. He was stabbed twice in the stomach. Who would do something like that? It seemed so unfair that we were here while Adele was out there somewhere and Dylan was dead.

I didn't go to the living room at three o'clock for tea, as Alan's mum had requested. The whole situation was stiff and uncomfortable. I called my mother instead.

'Why did you go there with him?' she demanded.

'As I said before, he invited me.'

'You could have said no, the whole situation is weird he's Adele's boyfriend. Why on earth does he want you there? Are you in a relationship with him?'

'No,' I said too loudly.

'Then what are you doing with him? How do you think her mother would react if she found out Adele's boyfriend whisked you away to Surrey?'

'Mum, Adele went missing and his friend was murdered this isn't easy on him either and he didn't whisk me away. We're friends.'

'Of course, it's not. I feel for the lad but I don't want you to be sucked into it.'

But I was already sucked into it. The banging on the door made me jump and I dropped the phone on the floor. I could hear my mum panicking.

Phoebe, are you okay? Phoebe!

'Come in,' I said in a sweet voice.

The door opened, Alan stepped in and I held out my hand to him.

I picked the phone off the floor. 'Mum, I'm fine, but I've got to go. Love you, I'll call you tomorrow.'

Alan's eyes were red as if he had been crying.

'Are you all right?'

'Ask me in ten years,' he said, 'You're ready?'

No. 'Yes.'

Chapter Twenty-seven

There were lemon cakes served with tea, the irony. A housekeeper was lurking about, and a man attended to the garden. No butler. Alan sat on the sofa across from me, his arms crossed defensively and he had a rather hostile look on his face. He wished for Adele to sit there instead of me and for an instant, I wondered if it had crossed his mind that I was the one who should have gone missing, not Adele. That somehow all of this was my fault, rowing with Adele so badly to the point it made her go missing and Dylan being murdered. I was the dead slug sitting on this plush sofa; the mouse infesting his mum's house.

'Finance,' Martha said. 'Do you plan to work for a big firm?'

'Yes. Maybe become an investment advisor, then open my own business,' I said, confident, sure of myself. My plans seemed so far away now.

Alan snapped a glance at me. How boring and unglamorous I sounded. Maybe I was a bland person studying for one of the most mundane, monotonous jobs. Nothing was dazzling about finance. I remembered why I was there, and it wasn't to impress his mother. She saw me as a girl who was going to pick a safe career where there was money involved. Sensible. Responsible. Boring.

'A businesswoman. Good,' she said.

Was that relief I heard in her voice? For a moment, I had an image of this happening over and over. A queue of girls meeting Alan's mother, all trying to win her approval. Adele would die trying. But no, there weren't queues of girls.

'Are you taking a break from your studies with all that's been going on?' she asked. 'Please, have a lemon cake.'

Martha offered me the tray of neatly cut cakes.

It was like having tea at the Ritz, not that I ever went, Martha must have though. I took a cake to be polite and placed it on my saucer.

'I am, yes, but I plan to go back soon.'

We all took a sip of our teas as if the whole thing was staged. Martha did most of the talking, merely asking questions to get to know me or trying to be nice to ease the awkwardness. I tried to think about what to say, but I couldn't think of anything. My mind was blank. Alan stared at the carpet, lost in thought.

'Do you play any instruments?' Martha asked.

'I'm afraid not.'

'All of my boys have been musically trained. I think it's an excellent skill to have. I have always been fascinated with musicians, it's so glamourous,' she beamed. 'Have you heard Alan play the piano? He's wonderful.'

'Mum...' Alan said, embarrassed.

'I have, yes,' I said. I turned to Alan. 'Would you take it up again?'

He looked up at the ceiling, irritated by my question. 'No.'

'Why not?' I insisted.

His stare was so cold I thought for a second it would turn me into a block of ice.

'Because I don't want to. I told you this,' he said irritably.

'He didn't enjoy being on stage. Alan likes to be behind the scenes, don't you, love?' Martha said.

Alan broke eye contact by looking at the grandfather clock.

A door banged shut.

'Peter,' Martha called out.

'Yep,' the newcomer said.

'We're here,' she announced.

Footsteps approached and a man in his fifties walked in. He was tall and lean, with greying hair, chiselled features, and blue eyes.

'Hey, Dad,' Alan said.

'Alan,' Peter said. 'So glad you're here finally.'

His father turned to me. 'Oh, you brought a friend with you, I see.'

'This is Phoebe,' Alan said.

His father did a double-take. 'You're the friend of the missing girl.'

The missing girl, not Adele, as if she didn't have an identity.

His father took a seat beside me. 'I'm so sorry, is there any news?'

'No.'

A barrage of questions was fired at me and I liked Martha for asking me simple things.

'Peter,' Martha said after he asked me about the twentieth question and Alan did nothing to stop him. 'Phoebe is here as our guest to take her mind off what is going on.' she reminded her husband.

After dinner during which Alan's parents did most of the talking while Alan and I sat beside each other; me eating the food, which was delicious. Did they have a personal chef? I couldn't picture Martha with her French manicure getting her hands dirty. Alan ate a few bits of his veggie dish.

'This house has six bedrooms not counting the master bedroom, and four bathrooms plus a shower room,' Martha explained, lifting her wine glass.

'And those people in the portraits, are they related to you?' I asked.

I had to keep the conversation going. Martha looked at me as if to tell me, *oh you poor sweet thing*. I knew nothing about fine art or art in general.

'No, dear,' she replied.

After dinner, I went to the shower room. I lathered myself with thick expensive shower gel that smelt of pepper and orange mixed with a hint of coriander.

When I left the room, I heard voices coming from downstairs. I leaned against the wall to avoid being seen.

'The funeral is in London,' Alan said.

'And you're going?' Martha asked.

'Dylan was my best friend, of course, I'm going.'

'And you're going to ask Phoebe to go along?' Peter asked.

'Yes, I will. She knew Dylan too.'

'I see,' Peter said.

'And there is still no news about Adele?' Martha asked.

'Nothing, I can't take it. Everything all at once,' Alan said, 'I miss her,'

'Was your relationship serious with Adele?' Peter asked.

'It was.'

'Oh Alan, first a woman ten years older than you with a twelve-year-old son then this Barbie doll, where did you get your terrible taste in women?' Martha said.

'Mum, Adele is missing and you don't know her,' he argued.

'I'm sorry, honey, but a guy like you, with your achievements, you can do so much better.'

Alan was in a relationship with an older woman who had a twelve-year-old son? Was this the woman he had a relationship with for four years?

'You can't talk like that about someone you haven't met. Adele is beautiful, bright, and funny,' Alan argued.

Had Alan forgotten Adele was seeing Greg behind his back? Adele would have milked him until the last drop if she'd seen all this wealth. Adele wasn't a gold digger but had no ambitions and would have been more than happy to settle for someone who provided for her while she provided the blow jobs. A small price to pay for what she would get. I sound like a bitch, but it was the truth.

'I know the type,' Martha said. 'Plenty of them around, girls who think they are special but they'll be ordinary, a carbon copy of the next. I'm sorry, I know you're fond of her, I just think you can do better and can't you think of anyone who has something to do with her going missing?'

'I can't,' Alan said.

'Is this the same girl you took to Edinburgh with you?' Peter asked.

'Yes.'

That explained the train ticket. Hannah and Janice said Adele mentioned nothing about going on a trip to Edinburgh. Why keep it a secret? Where did they stay? Was it a romantic trip, most probably to a five-star hotel sipping on champagne and having lots of wonderful sex? Alan treated Adele with luxury and she was cheating on him with Greg.

'Okay, Alan,' Peter said in a firmer tone. 'If you are so fond of Adele, can you tell me what the hell are you doing with her friend?'

'It's not that simple.'

'Not that simple?' Peter said exasperated. 'You brought her all the way here to this house. A friend of your missing girlfriend and you're telling me it's not that simple? These things are simple, it's a yes or no kind of situation. Have you stopped for a second to consider what it would look like to the police?'

'We are not suspects,' Alan said.

'Yet,' Peter reasoned.

'We're not sleeping together, so you have nothing to worry about,' Alan said.

'But the police don't know that,' Martha said.

'You're not sleeping with her? Then what the hell are you doing with her?' Peter asked.

'You can tell us, honey, if you are, we're not having illusions you're not having sex,' Martha said.

'Mum, please!'

'I think you need to take action,' Martha suggested.

'Like what?'

'The boyfriend is always a suspect in this situation,' Peter pointed out.

'Well, if I am, how come I'm not locked up in a cell?' Alan said confidently.

'Because they are gathering evidence against you. I think you should talk to a lawyer,' Peter said.

'A lawyer for what?' Alan asked, 'As for Phoebe, she is a friend, I enjoy her company. She's…'

'Beautiful?' Martha said.

'Whatever,' Alan said.

Martha thought I was beautiful?

'I see you with someone like Phoebe,' Martha said.

'What?'

'I don't see why not, she's pretty and sensible. She has her head on her shoulders. Clearly not a bimbo.'

'Don't make any wedding plans, Mum,' Alan said.

Alan was mourning, not only for Dylan but for Adele. Despite everything, he still missed her.

Chapter Twenty-eight

The next morning, I woke up early. The house was still and I didn't know what to do. I couldn't make myself at home, not when I was a guest. I got dressed and went for a walk. I wandered about on my own, not knowing where I was going then slipped while going down a slope. Between curses and getting back on my feet, my phone went off and it buzzed like it was having a heart attack from all the texts from Alan.

Where are you? The first text went.

The gardener said he saw you walking down the path. Please answer me when you get this text.

Why have you wandered off on your own?

Are you lost?

Should I send a search party looking for you?

I replied.

Went out for a walk. What's the urgency?

I could sense his annoyance and irritation from where I was.

There is no urgency I'm just wondering where you went.

Why?

I just want to know.

Alan's face was hard and tense when I found him sitting in the living room.

'What took you so long?' he demanded.

'I told you I went for a walk.'

'Next time inform someone, don't just take off.'

'It's not like I got lost.'

'It's just common courtesy to let people know your whereabouts,' he argued.

'Okay, I'm sorry. I won't do it again,' I said.

'Dylan's funeral is in two days,' he announced.

'Oh.' I tried to master a look of surprise. 'So, you're going back?'

'I'll go to the funeral and come back here. I need some time away from all of that nonsense.'

'I see.'

'What do you see?'

'Nothing.'

The whole conversation was ridiculous.

Alan moved closer to me. 'Is there a problem?'

'No problem,' I said.

'I suppose you're coming to the funeral.'

'Yes, I'll come. If you want me to that is.'

'I do.'

It dawned on me I had nothing proper to wear.

I stood in front of the full-length mirror, inspecting myself. I'd bought a black suit from Primark. It wasn't so bad and nobody was going to check the label anyway. Two cars were waiting outside. Alan's parents were coming to the funeral too. His brothers never made an appearance. Both had lots to do. Apparently more than being there for their brother. It seemed rather odd not to offer their support. I sat in the living room. The house was so quiet it was almost scary though sometimes there was a creak of the wood which I could never get used to. The housekeeper walked past and went on with her tasks, pretending I wasn't there. All of it was too strange. I stared at the piano, neglected in the corner. Since I had been here, not once had Alan used the piano. I'd thought he would drown his sorrows with it. What happened that made Alan quit? Was it because of Perry White? I doubted Alan was arsed about what a bitter man wrote about him in magazines and blogs. He wouldn't quit because a man talked shit about him. His death was mysterious though. A kinky game went wrong. The club came to mind; the whole set up of it. The eroticism it possessed. Did Perry go there? Did the police know about this secret club hidden under a dodgy sad-looking bar? Martha walked into the living room looking elegant in a suit. Unlike mine, it was Chanel.

'Phoebe,' Martha said.

In her hand was a crossbody bag, also Chanel. Peter came in shortly after, dressed in a black suit. We sat around the room waiting for Alan.

'What's taking so long?' Peter said, checking his watch.

A few minutes later, Alan appeared also smartly dressed in black.

'Finally,' Peter said, standing up and leaving the room.

Martha walked up to her son, fussing over him.

'We're going to be late. We'd better go,' she said.

Alan nodded.

As I suspected, we were travelling in separate cars. Alan wasn't chatty, but it was understandable, he was going to bury his friend.

'Thank you for being here,' Alan said.

'You're welcome.'

'It's selfish of me to make you come here and put your life on hold.'

'Well, you would have done the same for me,' I said.

Would he have done the same for me? I didn't second guess this, Alan had been there for me as much as I have for him. He lied to the police for me, and I couldn't work out why. I had so much to ask him yet I didn't want to upset him. His phone pinged. I turned my attention back to the window. The phone pings became background noise. Who was he texting? I opened the window and let the wind blow on my face, enjoying the slaps it gave me.

'Can you close the window?' he asked.

Was he afraid of ruining his hairstyle? I told the driver to put the radio on. *All By Myself* was playing. A few minutes later, Alan asked for the radio to be turned off.

Chapter Twenty-nine

As soon as I saw Dylan's picture on the altar, I couldn't help but tear up. He was dead and his killer was out there and there would be no justice until he or she was caught. I blended into the background as I didn't know anyone in there. Martha shook hands with a teary-eyed couple who I presumed were Dylan's parents. Alan walked over and the woman wrapped her arms around him and it was all too much. Peter was staring ahead, deep in thought, then looked at me and signalled for me to sit next to him. It was strange he didn't go to speak to Dylan's parents and pay his respects, or maybe he had and I hadn't noticed. The church was full of mourners and a priest dressed in white was reading from the Bible. I scanned the church, not knowing what I was looking for. Alan nudged me to keep still, as if I were a restless child. I was about to look at him when from the corner of my eye, I saw a woman on her feet standing at the back by the door. I did a double-take, my heart stopping for a second or two. It was the same woman I'd seen at the club and outside my apartment. I stood up and Alan looked up at me, his face aghast.

'Sit down,' he hissed under his breath.

'I'll be right back.'

I got a few displeased looks as I made my way through the church. If Alan's eyes were knives, he would have killed me right there. I looked at the people who were standing, but the woman didn't seem to be there anymore. She must have seen me getting up and left. I exited the church; black cars were parked along with the hearse. The drivers were outside, smoking, and they threw me several glances. No sign of her. I turned to go back inside and nearly crashed into Alan.

'What the fuck are you doing?' he said.

'Why're you out here?' Go back inside.'

'What are you doing?' he insisted.

'I…'

He grabbed me by the arm. 'You're being disrespectful, you know that?'

'I mean no disrespect.'

'Shut up and be quiet,' he snapped. 'I'm going to bury my best friend soon. Do you have any idea how painful all of this is?'

I said nothing to this. My cheeks went red with shame. He turned and stomped inside, ignoring me for the rest of the ceremony.

Outside, a girl rushed to Alan. She was tall with long blonde hair. She wrapped her arms around him.

'Baby, I'm so sorry,' she said planting two kisses on his cheeks.

I walked past them feeling Alan's hot angry gaze on me as I surveyed the street.

Nothing.

During the burial, I stayed in the car and watched from there. I didn't see Alan's parents; they must have gone home. All of it, the church and the burial was too personal and it wasn't my place. After it was over, Alan lingered for a bit, talking to Dylan's mother. Alan shook Dylan's father's hand, but he pulled him into a hug. The father was crying. Alan stomped to the car afterwards, still inflamed with temper. He ignited a cigarette and the car moved. I didn't dare to speak. How could I explain what I saw without sounding insane? I glanced at the window and felt holes burning through me.

'Why did you leave the church?' Alan asked in a much calmer voice.

'I'd rather not say,' I replied.

He huffed and puffed; a balloon of emotions ready to burst.

'Seriously? You'd rather not say?'

'No.'

'Tell me.'

'I saw her.'

'Who did you see?'

'The woman from the club.'

'You saw her at the church?' he asked in disbelief.

'See? You wouldn't believe me. You think I'm off my trolley.'

'I didn't say that, I just can't deal with this right now.'

The next day, I wandered around the house. Alan didn't talk to me for the rest of the day and didn't come down for dinner either. I heard Martha ask the housekeeper to prepare an extra plate of food and after she ate, she left and took the plate upstairs. Martha didn't come down until later, where I was browsing the collection of books.

'Have you been to the study?' Martha asked.

'No.'

'There are more books over there. It's by the foyer on the right-hand side.'

The study had a fireplace that hadn't been used for a long time and logs stood by it. Old hardbacks filled the shelves. A hardwood desk stood in the middle of the room, behind it a plush leather executive chair. There was a large globe, and artwork hung on the wall. I heard footsteps above me. Was that Alan's room? The wood complained. Was it him pacing up and down?

I ran my hand on the spines of books as I walked past then stopped and stared at a spine that stood out among the collection of old books. A black and white glossy hardback. There it was again, *Lost and Found*. What was the connection between this book and Alan? He had a copy in his apartment, Adele found it and bought it, and now it was here among the collection of books at his parents'.

The moon cast rays on the bed as I stared at the ceiling, listening to the occasional creaking of the house. It was faded with the sound of music coming from downstairs. I thought of Adele and me playing as children. Adele played with the dolls while I broke them. There were signs from the start who would be the girly one among us. The memories played like an old, faded photograph, from the time we went to Spain to celebrate passing our GCSEs, to the trip to Cyprus for her birthday. The laughter came to me powerfully, blocking out the piano downstairs. Why did everything escalate to shit? We'd had so many plans. Adele had said she'd be a model when she grew up and had the looks for it. While I said I'd like to be an astronaut. Neither of us became models or astronauts. They were childish dreams. Children dream of setting the world alight, but in the end, nobody does. Alan did though, a pianist, a virtuoso. Beautiful and highly accomplished and I was dull like my turtlenecks, grey, safe and pedestrian. I would end up in an office like the rest of them. I would work my way up and have the advantage of a reserved parking space if I were lucky. While Alan would go on leading this glamorous life though why was I comparing myself to him? I was in Surrey in this mansion of a house hearing Mozart playing downstairs only a floor separating us. If Alan didn't come into our lives, if I hadn't noticed him, Adele wouldn't have gone missing. I stood from the bed, unable to sleep, and looked out of the window at the gibbous moon. A few stars dotted the sky as the music went on, getting smoother now. The moon cast a reflection on the pool; a figure heading towards the shed. It could have been Martha or Peter. What was in that shed?

Alan's friends who lived in the area dropped by. It was the girl from the funeral and a guy was with her. Her name was Sherry and the guy was the boyfriend, Liam. We were out by the pool. Alan stayed as far away from me as possible, as if I had the plague, and I was getting annoyed with his behaviour. He had lost his friend, but it didn't excuse him for being so rude. Alan wasn't rude. Not exactly. Just distant. Frosty. I was here, away from everything I knew. My mum and Tom had called me about ten times, wanting to know my every move. How long would I be staying? My mum wanted to know if I needed time off; I was welcome to stay with her. It was the last place I wanted to be; I didn't want to face Adele's mother.

While Tom kept asking me why I was going into so much trouble for someone I barely knew?

Sherry was a hairstylist, the one who did the masterful work, her words not mine, in Alan's hair. I sat under the sun with my round, red-rimmed sunglasses. Questions demanded attention like why there was another copy of that damn book in the study? Why Alan quit being a pianist? Was the death of the music critic really a sex game gone wrong, or was it murder? If it was murder, who murdered him?

'How about we hang out the four of us?' Sherry suggested.

'That's a good idea, we should do it,' Liam said.

Alan remained quiet, blending into the shadows.

'How about tonight? You guys made any plans?' Sherry asked. 'It would be fun. We can go for drinks then hit a club.'

Alan's silence was black and heavy.

'I mean, what were you two going to do in this godawful big house by yourselves?' Liam said.

I was blinking behind my sunglasses. We weren't just the two of us, his parents were here.

Liam wiggled his eyebrows at Sherry then at Alan. Alan's silence continued to grow, in depth and in darkness.

'Your parents left, right?' Sherry asked Alan.

Alan sipped into his beer. 'Yes.'

Where did they go? How come nobody said anything? Why was I the last to know?

'Where did they go?' I asked Alan.

'They went to Edinburgh for the weekend. There's a tennis tournament my mum wanted to see,' he said.

'Edinburgh? Isn't that where you took Adele?' I asked.

If his eyes were a laser, they would have melted his Ray-Bans.

Chapter Thirty

After Sherry and Liam left, I walked into the house. Alan came after me.

'Is there something you have to tell me?' he said.

'No.'

'Then what the hell was that all about?' he snapped.

I sighed. 'I'm sure you've seen the train ticket I found in Adele's room,'

'Yeah, so, what about it?'

'Why didn't you tell me you took her to Edinburgh?'

'Because it's none of your business, that's why,' he retorted. 'Adele and I were in a relationship. It seems unusual to you, but that's what people in relationships do, they take trips. Stop rubbing Adele in my face,'

'Adele cheated on you,' I pointed out.

'She's still missing, she could be dead for all I know and you don't even give a shit.'

'I do give a shit.'

He ran his fingers through his hair in frustration. 'You sure have a funny way of showing it.'

'I had nothing to do with her going missing,' I said.

'I know you didn't,' he said, calmer now. 'Look, Phoebe, I'm trying to be nice to you.'

'I don't want your pity.'

He looked at me as if I'd insulted each member of his family. 'I'm not pitying you.'

I raised my hand to stop him from talking. 'Shut up, shut up, just *shut up*.'

I spent the rest of the day painting my nails. First red; I stopped and admired my work then I removed it and tried the black, then blue, remove and repeat. I read for a bit and when it got dark, the slam of a car door came from outside followed by the hum of an engine. I got up from the bed and a posh black Audi A1 was driving away. Was that Alan? Did he leave me alone in this house? Maybe he went to a run an errand, I thought, or went to get us some food, although he could have ordered it. I left the bedroom; all the lights were off in the house. I had a bath and lay there for a long time emptying my mind. I blow-dried my hair and packed my suitcase. Alan wasn't back yet. I gazed out of the window at the shed.

The floorboards groaned as I descended the stairs. I went to the kitchen and poured myself a glass of water. The house was so silent, it gave me the creeps. I left, shutting the door behind me and remembered that I didn't have a key and I'd locked myself out. I didn't have my phone on me either.

'Okay,' I said to myself. 'There has to be a back door somewhere.'

The cold crashed into my bones and I scuttled towards the shed. Droplets of rain landed on my head. Great, it was starting to rain. I'd locked myself outside and I was naked apart from a robe. I opened the door and fumbled for the light. There didn't seem to be one. I let my eyes adjust to the darkness. I made out a string and pulled it, and a light bulb went on. It wasn't a tool shed as I'd expected, more like a storage room. There were boxes stacked neatly on the shelves along with cans of paint. There was what looked to be a worktop. A large box in the middle. I moved closer, careful of what to touch. I didn't know what kind of creepy crawlies were in there. A clap of thunder rolled outside, making me jump. What did I expect to find anyway? A dead body? It was better to find a way back inside the house before Alan came back and wondered where I'd gone off to, and I didn't want him to catch me running about in the house grounds in a bathrobe either.

Somehow something compelled me to look further. The big box was taped. I ignored it and went to the shelves and rummaged through. Most of the boxes contained junk and old clothes. In the next box were a set of photographs. I pulled them out. The first one was of a teenage boy with long hair wearing an oversized white jumper. It was of Alan. I glanced over my shoulder as the rain knocked against the windows. I flipped to another photo. This one was of a woman with short hair, beside her stood a young boy about eleven or twelve. Behind them was a fountain. I flipped the photo over but there was nothing written. Something told me to stop poking around and find a way back in the house, but the urge to keep on looking was irresistible. Something was hidden here; not sure what. I listened to my logical sense and put everything back where it had been. Alan had been gone a long time and was most probably on his way or already at the house wondering where I was. Would he go to my room and find my luggage all packed and ready to go? The rain tapped against the wood, the door opened and Alan walked in.

Chapter Thirty-one

The look on his face wasn't of anger but amusement, maybe irritation. I wracked my brain, looking for an excuse. I was snooping in his mother's shed. He looked down at my bare feet and raised an eyebrow.

'I locked myself out,' I said. 'I came here to shield myself from the rain.'

It came out automatically, and it wasn't a complete lie.

'I know, I'd been looking for you,' he said. 'I saw the light on.'

I couldn't read his expression and didn't know if he believed me or not. He took a step closer to me and I didn't move. I kept gazing up at him, taking him in. His eyes were cold, but there was something else in them, tenderness? Affection? No, hunger.

'I'm sorry,' he whispered, putting his hands on my waist. 'I have been awful to you these past few days.'

He had been but I was too exhausted to argue with him so I said nothing.

He pressed his body against mine. There was a tightening in my chest. He kissed me in a way that he wanted me to feel him. How he felt. It was so sensual and erotic. The robe fell open and he pressed me against the shelf. The rain was hammering on the shed furiously. He lowered himself and I gasped and shut my eyes, grabbing the shelf. He stood again and I removed his jacket, let it drop to the floor and undid the belt of his jeans. Within minutes, I had my legs wrapped around him. Feeling him. Owning him. He stopped, his cheeks flushed. He grabbed my robe and laid it on the floor and lay me down on it. My hands were all over him as I felt his weight on top of me, no longer worried about the creepy crawlies that lingered in that shed. We had sex. Fucked. Made love, whatever it was. Maybe all three combined into one. I wrapped my legs around him, burying him further like quicksand. I was lava. I was love.

Afterwards, he got dressed and I put back my robe, which had splotches of dirt on it. The silence was ominous. Alan had his back to me and the flicker of the lighter pierced the shed. He picked his leather jacket from the floor and put it on with his cigarette dangling from his mouth. He puffed and his eyes went through me and the way he looked at me, it was so frosty, as if he was angry at me about something. My brain ticked, trying to work out why. Maybe because he'd found me here and knew I was sticking my nose in places it didn't belong. Maybe he had something hidden here, or maybe because of what just happened. He was the one who started it. It amazed me how a man and woman can connect with such power and intensity. To share that kind of passion, crossing the barrier between skin and flesh then hating each other the next. The whole thing was direct, unsentimental. He walked to the door meaning it was time to leave. The rain had stopped and the grass, apart from being wet, was cold under my feet. He unlocked the front door and I followed him inside, still not saying a word. Alan pulled me against the door as he slammed it closed with a thud which vibrated through the quiet, large house. We stared at each other then he kissed me.

'You need a fresh robe,' he said.

Alan walked away and came back holding a clean robe.

'I'm leaving tomorrow,' I said.

There was a momentary silence.

'Okay,' he said.

I felt hurt by this response, and I didn't know why. What did I expect, that he'd beg me to stay? That we spend the night together?

I walked past him and reached the stairs, then I turned, Alan was standing there looking sheepish.

'Don't you feel you betrayed Adele?'

'Why? Adele didn't think twice of betraying me,' he remarked.

Great. I was the revenge fuck now. He did it to get back at her. What about me? I stopped him when we were in his apartment, but I didn't hear myself say no this time.

'But she didn't betray you with your friend,' I said. 'How would you feel if a friend did that to you?'

'None of my friends would do that to me, but they aren't exactly real friends. My true friend was Dylan,' Alan said sadly.

'I'm so sorry.'

He sighed. 'I don't want to think about Adele right now. I just want to be alone. Goodnight, Phoebe, I'll see you in the morning.'

In the morning, Alan was in the kitchen nursing a cup of coffee. He poured me a cup and went back to whoever he was texting on his phone. I didn't know if he was avoiding the situation, but it made things awkward between us. How would I feel if I found out while I had been missing, my boyfriend and my friend started shagging? I wouldn't be too thrilled about it.

'I called you a taxi,' he said.

He couldn't wait to see the back of me or was being a gentleman, I didn't know which. After I drank my coffee, I stood up with the excuse that I have to pack my already packed suitcase.

'I don't regret it,' he said.

I glanced back at him. Alan sipped his coffee, 'Do you?'

'I need time to process all of this.'

When the taxi arrived half an hour later, Alan opened the door then closed it again. He pressed his lips together; his eyes hidden beneath his long eyelashes. It was like he had a hard time making up his mind about something.

'I should tell that taxi driver to go back and you stay here with me.'

'Alan…'

He kissed me with such passion my legs melted into water.

'Something to think about,' he said and opened the door.

I left, wondering where this would go. What this made us? Arseholes, that was for sure. What were we doing?

I had been hesitant to go into the apartment, not knowing what to expect. I inspected each room with a heavy heart. But it seemed fine, nothing was replaced or missing. There was one thing I had to do, talk to Greg. He was staying at his parents' but I didn't know where they lived. I could send him a message on Facebook but then I decided not to. I contacted Janice instead.

Me: *Has Greg returned?*

Janice: *Hey, I came by your apartment, but no one was there.*

Me: *I went away for a while.'*

Janice. *Cool.*

Me: *Why did you come over to my place?*

Janice: *To tell you about Greg, that he's back.*

Couldn't she text me rather than coming here?

Me: *Cheers.*
Janice: *Wait, are you going to speak to him?*
Me: *Why would I do that?*

It was exactly what I was going to do. I tried my luck with YouTube hoping I would find clips of Alan when he was Allan Styles but again nothing.

The awfulness, the confusion and the hurt led us to this path. Alan made it sound as he seduced me out of revenge, but I didn't think it was that. He was just hurt and lonely. I was the same. Somehow this filled me with panic. Despite everything, even if it was wrong, I wanted more, because he was more.

Chapter Thirty-two

I didn't have a plan as I stood outside the university main gate. I couldn't go in because Hannah and Janice would see me. I had to speak to Greg and to do that; it had to be outside the building. I had access to the timetable. So, I waited, if he was there at all. I could have sent a message to Janice, but she could tell Greg and I didn't want her to know I was there anyway. So, I stalked my university and there was a creeping sensation like a bug crawling on my skin that I was being watched. My eyes darted around the street, but no one was there. Around forty-five minutes later, students started coming out. I spotted Greg among the crowd, tall and lanky with his straw hair spiked up. Greg hurried his pace as if he were in a rush to get somewhere, his head down, not interacting with anyone. Greg wasn't the most popular, but he had his circle of friends. I stayed behind him so I wouldn't be seen, but kept my eyes on him. Greg entered Pret A Manger. He ordered a coffee by the counter and sat down by the window.

The look on his face was priceless when he saw me walking to his table. He looked around, but the patrons were too engaged in their lives to take notice of a girl with long black hair and a black coat walking in.

'Hello, Greg,' I said, sitting across from him.

His eyes went wide. 'Phoebe, what are you doing here?'

'I came here for you.'

'I'm flattered.'

'I'm not here to flatter you.'

'Of course not.'

'I heard what happened,' I said.

He tore open the packet of sugar. 'Yes, and you're here to ask me about Adele, is that it? I've already told the police what I know.'

'But you haven't told me.'

He sighed. 'I was seeing her in secret... for a few months, then she met Alan and, I don't know, it was different.'

'How?' I asked.

Greg poured sugar into his cup. 'Shouldn't you order something?'

'I'm fine,' I said.

He stirred his coffee. 'I don't know, it was strange. Adele had an issue with you being into Alan, wanted you out of the picture. I don't know how to say this...'

I knew what he was going to say.

'Adele wanted me to invite you to the party okay, and the rest.'

'Well, Adele wasn't the most excellent of friends,' I remarked.

'Adele is jealous of you.'

My mouth gaped open. 'Adele jealous of me? Are you trying to have a laugh?'

'I don't know if I can laugh anymore. Adele hated that she's bangable but you're beautiful. Composed and in control, you know… Sure of yourself.'

'So, you're telling me Adele ran away because of this?'

'No, I didn't know Adele planned to run away. She said nothing to me.'

'So, you're no longer a suspect?' I asked.

He glared at me. 'I wouldn't be here now, would I? Are you in touch with Alan?'

'Why would I be?'

'Because Adele is out of the picture, I thought… anyway it's weird. I looked him up; he's like, he doesn't even exist. I don't know how the police don't find it suspicious. But he wasn't a suspect because he has alibis. I would be careful if I were you.'

'You think he had something to do with Adele going missing?'

He leaned closer. 'Tell me, Phoebe, leaving aside the infatuation you and Adele had with him, what do you know about him?'

Now Greg sounded like my brother.

'Phoebe, he's playing you both. Adele, well… she wasn't the sharpest tool in the shed but you… I thought you were better than this but take a good-looking guy and the right words and everything goes out the window.'

'What are you talking about?'

'Just be careful, that's all I have to say.'

After the meeting with Greg, which left me uneasy and rather unsettled. I took the route back to my apartment, glancing over my shoulder with my heart hammering against my chest. I had this feeling. An instinct that someone was following me. I increased my pace, my blood pulsing in my veins. People flew past me as the London traffic howled in my ears. I stopped by a traffic light and pressed the button as other people waited with me. I looked at them, the man in the navy-blue suit talking on his phone, the girl next to me with pink hair, not so much older than me, scrolling through Facebook. Nothing suspicious, no woman who looks like me. The light changed. I reached the pavement and quickened my pace with the key ready in hand. I looked over my shoulder. I'm being paranoid. I took a step forward and crashed into someone. A strange sound came out of my mouth between a cry and a scream. Alan was glancing down at me, his hands placed on my shoulders as if he was holding me in place.

When had he got back from Surrey? Why did he say nothing about coming back? Tom's and Greg's voices echoed in my head. *What do you know about him?* Strange things surrounded Alan. Adele going missing, changing his name, the dead journalist and Dylan being killed. Was it Alan following me? But Alan had come from the other direction, but he could have easily changed course to make it look like he was coming from the other way. He wasn't the enemy, was he?

'You're shaking,' he said.

I shook myself free from his grasp. 'When did you get back?'

'Just now.'

'Just now? And where were you going?'

The question sounded accusatory.

He squinted at me. 'What?'

'Where are you going?'

'Phoebe, what are you on about?'

'Just tell me where. I want to know.'

'I was going to work.'

I blinked at him, not believing him.

'Why are you so spooked? Where were you?'

'I went to run an errand,' I said.

Alan took my arm and led me to the apartment. I didn't like how I was around him. The same as—Adele. As if he were this unknown drug that made me high and paranoid at the same time. He took my keys from my hands and opened the door.

I sat on the sofa and Alan went into the kitchen and poured me a glass of water.

'Why is there nothing about you on the internet? Why did you quit playing the piano?' I asked before I could stop myself.

I couldn't hold it any longer. Alan looked back at me, no hint of surprise on his face.

At least the rest didn't come out. What I knew. His real name. The dead journalist. His mother owing a copy of *Lost and Found* in her study. Alan came towards me holding the glass of water and placed it down on the coffee table and sat across from me.

'I thought my mum told you why I quit. I didn't enjoy playing the piano,' he said. 'But I'll tell you everything, Phoebe.'

Every time he said my name, it sounded strange. As if it weren't my name, but someone else's. I waited.

He stood. 'Not now, I have to go to work.'

'When?' I asked, unable to mask the curiosity in my voice.

'Tonight. Over dinner.'

'Dinner?'

'Yes, a place where there are table and chairs where people go to eat,' he said.

He had such a way of making people feel like idiots.

'Don't patronise me,' I snapped.

'I will tell you tonight. Be ready at eight. Wait for me outside.'

How am I supposed to know he'll tell me the truth?

Chapter Thirty-three

We sat across from each other in a dimly lit restaurant with soft music playing and a waitress hovering around us. Alan shouldn't have gone to the trouble, a pub with beers and snacks would have been enough. I took a sip of water while Alan played with the fork. I opened my mouth to speak, but the waitress walked over with the wine. She was staring at Alan as she poured some wine for him to try. He played along, tasted the wine, told her it was fine, and she batted her eyelashes at him. As if she remembered he wasn't alone, she poured wine into my glass. Alan thanked her politely and she told him he was very welcome in a flirtatious tone before walking off, glancing at him over her shoulder. I knew what she was thinking, what is that stunner doing with her?

'So, you looked me up?' he asked.

My cheeks grew hot. 'Isn't that what people do?'

'Is it? I didn't look you up if you're wondering.'

'Well... I... got.'

'Curious?'

'Yes.'

The waitress showed up again, her eyes reserved only for him.

'Are you ready to order?' she asked in a sing-song tone. We hadn't opened our menus yet.

'We need more time,' Alan said, leaning back in the chair then reaching over for my hand and taking it in his.

'You found nothing because I changed my name,' he said in a low voice. 'As my mum told you, she wanted us to be musically trained. By the age of six, I was taking piano lessons. When I was eight, she made me take the clarinet and drums. My brothers had taken violin and guitar lessons. I didn't know if she had a plan to form a band but I developed a love for the piano. So, I quit the clarinet and drums and put all of my focus on that. I had to study and do homework as well. By the age of fifteen, I was already performing in theatres and studied music after that. I enjoyed it. Loved it actually, to travel at a young age and perform for people who paid money to see me play.' He paused and took a sip of wine as he went on holding my hand. I watched the long, slender fingers dance across my skin.

'Everything was going smoothly until there was this guy... this journalist who used to write stuff about me. Making remarks about my playing, which was fine, I mean it's not like I cared... I ignored him. Journalists write lots of stuff anyway, but it got weird.'

'Weird?' I asked.

'Yeah… it's like he developed this love and hate relationship with me. I didn't know him. He made it his business to be there when I performed. My mum was my manager at the time and she knew what was going on. He requested an interview which I refused. It got out of hand.' He shook his head. 'My mum had to file a restraining order against him. It's like I became an obsession of his.'

With each passing sentence, my blood turned colder and colder.

'It ruined the experience for me. I took a six-month break after that to think it through, to see if I felt the same way, if I should remain a pianist or do something else.'

'What did you do in those six months?'

'I produced albums for bands and artists. I found peace in it really. After six months I still felt the same way so I quit.'

'So, you quit because the journalist was stalking you?'

'That was part of it… then he died. You can look him up his name is Perry White. You'll find what you need to know about him.'

'How did he die?'

I had to act the part.

'He liked cocaine and extreme fetishes, which were what led to his demise.'

There was a hint of coldness in his tone. Alan wasn't sorry Perry White was dead; like a burden had been lifted off his shoulders. Alan fell quiet after that, and the flirty waitress came to take our order. We still hadn't looked at the menu, so Alan again told her to come back in ten minutes.

'Would you go back to it?'

'Piano?'

'Yes.'

He glanced down at the floor. 'I don't know. I've told no one about this.'

'No?'

'No...' he said and stared at me. 'I haven't told Adele either. She wasn't interested, to be honest. Now that I think about it, you were right.'

'About what?'

'That Adele wasn't interested in me as a person but more interested in well... you know...'

He cast me a shy glance.

'Why me then?' I asked.

He held my gaze. 'I don't know... after what we have been through, I trust you, I guess.'

What would happen when Adele comes back? Would he go back to her? There was that hole in the pit of my stomach. A desperate sort of feeling. Clingy and pathetic. I wasn't that sort of person, and I didn't know what was happening to me. After dinner, I didn't ask him to come up, so Alan and I went our separate ways.

I met Tom and we went for a walk to the market and he bought me a scarf. Afterwards, we went for lunch.

'We'll be going to Rome in three weeks,' Tom announced after we ordered.

'That's great. It's going to be amazing. Holly will love it,' I said.

'I hope so,' he said.

'Don't tell me you're still worried she'll say no?'

'You never know, do you? What if she's not ready?

'You're being paranoid, of course, she will say yes.'

'How can you be sure? Lots of people who were in a relationship said no when proposed to.'

'Tom, it will be fine, you'll see.'

He cut a piece of bread and dipped it into olive oil. 'How are things at your end?'

'Well, it has been…' I trailed off. I couldn't say good.

Adele hadn't been found and I hadn't figured who wrote that book, who had been coming in the flat, nor who that woman was.

'Tell me about Surrey, how it went?' Tom said. 'I know you told me on the phone but it was brief and Mum was so worried.'

'I know, but it was… fine.'

'You going off with your friend's boyfriend is fine? It's unethical if you ask me.'

'Unethical? Adele hadn't exactly been following the book of ethics. Alan's friend had been murdered… he was devastated.'

'I know… but still… how would Adele feel if she found out you had gone away together?'

'We didn't go away on a romantic trip. He invited me to his parents' house for God's sake. Adele should have thought about the consequences before cheating on him.'

Tom looked at me over the rim of the glass. Did he suspect something was going on between me and Alan?

I picked up the mail before going into the flat then inspected the apartment to make sure nothing weird had occurred. It looked fine, exactly as I'd left it. I put the kettle on and went through the mail. Junk mostly. The kettle boiled and I made a cup of coffee. On the floor was a white envelope. It must have dropped while I was going through the mail. I turned it over; three words were typed making my heart roll into my rib cage and my skin crawl.

Lost and Found.

Chapter Thirty-four

My hands were shaking so much, I struggled to open the envelope. I took deep breaths, counting to ten and then back to level out the anxiety. I tore the envelope and stared at the words, dismayed. Just a date and the address of a hotel in Mayfair. Why Mayfair of all places? I let the letter drop on the floor. *Lost and Found. Found and Lost.* I paced up and down and, in my head, I chanted *Lost and Found. Found and Lost.* It went on and on. I grabbed Adele's copy of the book as the true terror sank in of what this was. It was a re-enactment of the story. An act. A play. I was the sister looking for her lost brother. I folded the letter and placed it inside the book and stuffed it in my bag.

I had a long bath and stayed there until the water turned cold and goosebumps grew on my skin. I heard my phone ping several times. I blow-dried my hair and around nine o'clock Alan walked in using the key. I contemplated if I should tell Alan about the letter or not. Should I tell him I'd got a letter with the words *Lost and Found* just like the book?

I knew what I wanted and I was going to get it. I wasn't in the mood to talk, I just wanted him. What he could do for me. I had become Adele, interested in him because of his looks, for what lay between his legs. He was the cause of this; it was his fault. It's like he planned this. Alan followed me to the bedroom and I stood before him. I removed my bathrobe and stood naked in the familiarity of my room. I kissed him and slid the jacket off his shoulder. He whispered my name.

'Shhh,' I said.

I unbuttoned his shirt and went on my knees, hungry. My hands greedily undoing his belt. I was afraid and needed something to forget. I didn't tell him because I didn't know if I could trust him with something so explosive. I looked up at him, I was the cat now. A cat looking at the goldfish in a bowl. Only the goldfish had teeth.

I sat in the hotel lobby with my stomach churning. I didn't know what to expect. My eyes darted around the lobby and I looked up each time someone walked in. I ordered a pot of tea, but I hadn't touched it. I had been there for twenty minutes already and no one had arrived or maybe Adele was watching me but would not make an appearance. It was embarrassing; the people there must have thought I was on a date or a meeting, but the person didn't turn up. I waited and waited, then I stood and went to the bathroom, avoiding making eye contact with anyone. In the stall, I checked my phone. No messages. Nothing. Not even from Alan. Maybe someone wanted to play a stupid prank on me, sending me out there to waste my time, and it wasn't even funny. Did I think Adele would turn up here in a swanky hotel where people could recognise her? How deep did my level of stupid go? Angry with myself, I left the bathroom. Perhaps it wasn't Adele doing this at all. But someone else who had read the book? Alan. Would Alan do this to me? His mum? I walked back to the lobby to collect my belongings and get out of there.

'Phoebe, what are you doing here?'

I glanced up; it was Tom. He wore a suit and his laptop case with the red strap hung on his shoulder. He looked slightly dishevelled. His tie was loose and his hair was rumpled with a two-day-old stubble decorating his face.

'Tom!' I said, almost too loud.

He dropped his case down on the floor. 'Are you all right? You look upset.'

'No, I'm fine,' I lied. 'I went for a walk and came in here to get a cup of tea.'

'You went for a walk on your own.'

'Yeah, what's so odd about that?'

'Phoebe... are you looking for Adele?'

What a strange question. What makes him think I was looking for Adele in a posh hotel?

'What are you doing here?'

'I manage the IT at this hotel. They are one of our clients.'

'Oh,' I said, sinking into the armchair.

I had the impulse to tell him everything about the woman I'd seen dressed like me, the letter I'd received, the book *Lost and Found* that Alan, Adele and his mum had copies of. Someone breaking into my apartment. I couldn't hold it any longer, and I needed someone to confide in.

'You should stay at Mum's, for a while. This is putting a lot of strain on you and it's beginning to show. You can't pretend everything is normal when it isn't.'

'What do you want me to do? Put my life on hold? I already have.'

Tom ordered two pots of tea from the waiter.

'I mean, it will help. You can rest for a bit.'

The waiter arrived, placed the teas on the table and removed the untouched tea I'd ordered earlier.

'Here, have some tea it will soothe your nerves,' Tom said pouring tea in the cup and handing it to me.

'I thought you said you were going to Rome?'

He stared at me and I couldn't read his expression. This is my brother. We share the same blood. We have a bond. A strong connection yet, I couldn't read him. It was like I didn't know him. Why did I feel that way?

'I am. In two weeks.'

'In time for my birthday,' I said.

'I'll get you something from Rome,' he said. 'Now drink up and I'll take you home.'

'No need, you're working. I shouldn't bother you, I'm fine.'

'Work can wait, you are more important.'

To occupy my time and to give myself something to do, I cooked and went over the afternoon's events. Running into Tom at the very same hotel that was mentioned in the letter. Did he send it? Why would my brother send me a letter with the words *Lost and Found* on the envelope?

Alan came over half an hour later looking like a five-star hotel. It was all about him. Everything was about him. He was the maker of this fuckery. This campaign was about him. Adele and I were the buffoons submitting to his power. He was the male magic we couldn't escape, so deep our obsession was for him. So blinded we were, we would have walked straight into a wall. Endless his campaign was. He asked me how my day had gone and kissed me on the cheek. He saw the pans and pots on the kitchen counter and looked at me with one eyebrow raised.

'I'm cooking dinner, care to join me?'

'I would love to.'

I made up some bogus story of where I'd been when what I wanted to tell him was, *Alan, I got a letter with the words Lost and Found*. I didn't tell him that. I poured him a glass of wine instead. We clinked the glasses together and drank and he told me about his mother, how she wanted him to go back to Surrey. I turned and chopped the tomatoes. He came behind me and his hand reached the handle of the knife. He smelt my hair and nibbled my ear then nuzzled my neck and I offered it to him as if he were a God. Both of our hands were still holding the knife. His free hand fiddled with the waistband of my leggings. He eased them off together with my underwear. His heat became my heat and we still held the knife by the handle. I let him tear me apart knowing that afterwards, he would restore me. There was a loud thud on the floor of the chopping board. Tomatoes decorated the floor like red balls. Some of them had squashed leaving red marks like blood, the pips like intestines. I collected them afterwards and Alan went to the bathroom and it still didn't feel like it was enough. It was a place where food is prepared for a different kind of art, and we had painted that kitchen with our art. I was getting what I wanted and he had given it to me so willingly. I had the pleasure but I never understood the longing. As long he was around; I had no peace. Was it the same for Adele? Was this how she felt? Alan came out of the bathroom and I was still a blob of mess. My brain yelled at me I was an arsehole for doing this.

'Thanks for helping,' I said.

'You're welcome.'

If I hadn't laid my eyes on Alan, Adele would still be here. We would go on with our cracked friendship being roommates and maybe after we graduated, we would have parted ways or lost touch.

I typed Perry White and Allan Styles restraining order into Google, which led me to a big fat nothing. Maybe his mother did everything in her power to keep this from going to the press.

There was a missing piece of the puzzle. Alan quitting from being a concert pianist to become a producer, changing his name, the journalist who hated him, stalked him so there was a restraining order, to the journalist dying in mysterious circumstances. How all this connected to Adele, I didn't know. Adele went missing based on that book, *Lost and Found*. There was the question of who wrote it, and why there was a copy at Martha's house.

Chapter Thirty-five

It was my birthday in a few days and I have told no one about it. Well, not no one—Alan. I had been avoiding him for the past few days. It was for the best to stay away from him for a while. I was rotten with guilt for Adele going missing and now for what I was doing with Alan. It was wrong, even if Adele had done terrible things.

A knock came on the door when I was preparing a sandwich to eat in front of the telly.

'Great. You're alive,' Alan said and turned to leave.

'I'm sorry for not returning any of your texts and calls. I just wanted to be alone,' I said.

'You should have said so,' he said.

'I know. Can you stay with me?'

'Oh, now you want my company?'

'I do.'

What are you saying? My brain screamed at me.

I ended up telling him it was my birthday soon.

On the day, Alan sent me a text to wish me a happy birthday. He told me to be ready at eight pm. I didn't want to celebrate, it seemed wrong to do so. But he insisted.

I walked to the window with the dress that I was going to wear and parted the curtains. Alan stood in the living room, his back to the window. He wasn't alone. Someone was there with him. A woman, but I couldn't tell who; he was blocking the person. From the hand gestures, he seemed upset about something. I closed the curtain to avoid being seen and made a gap large enough for me to peek. Alan lifted his hand in anger. Who was that woman? His mum? Adele? The woman came into view slightly, but her back was to Alan, a purple hoodie covering her hair. She walked to the door. As she left, Alan turned towards the window and I moved away. What was going on? Who was that woman? Who could she be? What else was he hiding?

Tom sent me a text wishing me a happy birthday and sent me a picture of him and Holly in Rome with a caption that read:

She said yes. We are engaged!!!

I beamed with pride. I got more texts from my mum and dad. Janice had sent me a text, so did Greg.

Alan came over and didn't look upset. If he were, he was good at hiding it.

I wanted to feel like myself. To have a sense of normality, but nothing about this felt normal. Too much had happened and Adele still lingered between us. We shouldn't be doing this, but here we were, him taking me out for dinner for my birthday as if we were a boyfriend and girlfriend. What it would look like to the police? What would Marion say about this? My parents and Tom? We sat in a nice restaurant similar to the one Adele took me to. It seemed so faded, that memory, like it was ages ago.

'Did you suggest to Adele to take me out to dinner after she started seeing you?' I asked.

'What?'

'Did you?'

'No, she wanted to.'

'But you gave her the money to pay for it. I mean she couldn't afford it.'

'I did, yes.'

'Why?'

'Because that's what people do.'

'You mean that's what boyfriends do.'

He searched my face. 'Is there a problem?'

'No, I'm just curious.'

He reached for the glass of wine and I did the same.

'Is there something you want to tell me?'

There was so much I wanted to tell Alan, the problem was from where to start?

'I think…' I trailed off.

'Yes?'

'…I'm thinking about Adele a lot,' I said.

Why wouldn't she come home? Someone was out there, a woman disguising herself as me, but it wasn't Adele. Who was it? Who would want to wish me harm?

'I think about her too,' he said.

The lights were low in the restaurant and people were talking, some eating, some barely touching their food. Three businessmen were arguing about who was going to pay the bill. I didn't know what I was looking for. It was my birthday; Adele would try to get in touch. How I didn't know. Adele always fussed on birthdays and made it her business to celebrate mine. Always had something planned: spas, shopping trips, weekend trips and parties, while what I wanted to do was curl up on the sofa, order a pizza, and open a bottle of wine.

'Do you think you and Adele would have lasted?' I asked.

His eyes were heavy on me. 'I don't think we would have, that the candle would have died in the end, and after what I found out about her, her being unfaithful...'

He was the flame, and she was the kindle of that flame. Was I the same?

'So, you're saying you and Adele would be over if she comes back?'

'I wouldn't resume the relationship, no. Why are we even talking about Adele? It's supposed to be all about you tonight.'

He leaned in closer, placing his arm around the chair and his other free hand glided to my thigh making my body tense. If anyone looked, they would have seen a loved-up couple in a blossoming relationship who couldn't keep their hands off each other. The beginning stages where everything was easy, fluffy, and nice with no idea what they were getting themselves into.

Chapter Thirty-six

I woke up in the middle of the night. At first, I couldn't recognise where I was. The moonlight illuminated the room. Alan lay asleep beside me. I dragged off the covers trying not to wake him, gathered my clothes and got dressed. I could have spent the night with him, but I wanted to be on my own and sleep in my own bed.

It sat innocently and prettily, a blue cupcake without a candle with a small envelope next to it. I stared at it in disbelief as my body rattled with fear. Did someone break-in? Couldn't be Alan, he was with me. It has to be Adele.

'Adele!' I shouted.

I waited for the reply, but of course, none came. I stalked to the coffee table and tore the envelope open.

Happy Birthday, Bitch!

I dropped the note and reached for my phone. My body worked on autopilot, knowing exactly what to do. I dialled DC Nash's number. My voice was calm as I told her to come over. I opened the curtains to check Alan's apartment. The curtains were closed and there didn't seem to be any lights on. Why should there be? He was asleep and didn't know I had left. I could have called him but I didn't want to involve him; this was between Adele and me. It was always between me and her. He was just the guy caught in the middle of our sick, twisted friendship. Somehow the prospect didn't terrify me, as if I wanted her to come and put an end to the madness she had created. I couldn't go on blaming Alan. He was the bloke I'd had a crush on and Adele got to him to spite me. None of this would have happened if I hadn't told her about him.

The buzzer went off and I saw Nash alone. I buzzed her in and waited for the knock on the door to come. It was a long wait but five minutes later it came. I opened the door and Nash had a strange look upon her face, like it was contorted with pain.

'Detective, are you all right?'

A weird sound came out of her mouth. Nash toppled on the floor and I threw my hands to my mouth to prevent myself from yelping as the detective lay by my feet, blood spreading across the floor, so red it looked almost black. My face went white as Janice stood before me, wearing her hair like mine, holding a bloody butcher's knife. I took a step backwards as Janice aimed the knife at me.

'Drag her inside,' Janice demanded.

I bent down, my heart thundering in my chest and sweat breaking at my temples, and dragged Nash by the feet and pulled her into the flat, leaving a trail of blood. I couldn't tell if she was still alive or not, but Janice had stabbed her in the back.

'Clean it up,' Janice said, gesturing with the bloodied knife.

She followed me to the kitchen and I reached for the roll of paper towels and cleaned up the blood.

My mind raced; it had been Janice all along. She was the one coming into the apartment, opening the curtains, fucking with my head. The woman dressed like me, that was her too. Did she have something to do with Adele disappearing? Why? She was her friend, what motive did she have? I grabbed another handful of paper towels and wiped the blood off, glossing my hand with red. Janice instructed me to throw away the paper napkins and wash my hands. Did she think she would get away with this? I washed my hands and blood flowed down the drain. My eyes went to the knife block and one knife was missing. Acid rose into my throat.

'Janice,' I began.

'Shut up,' she said. 'You will not get to talk,'

'It's my birthday, technically, I do whatever I want,' I said.

'Don't be smart, Phoebe. It has always been a pet peeve of mine about you, a smart mouth. Sit down.'

She gestured with her knife towards the sofa.

'I bet you're curious how I got the key to come in.'

I stared at her, not giving her a reply.

'Adele gave me a copy, well to Hannah technically, just in case of emergency. It was pretty convenient.'

Did Adele give a copy of this apartment key to Hannah? Why did she have to be so stupid, handing keys over as if it were a hotel room?

'Why?' I asked.

'You wanted Adele out of the picture so you could get your hands on *him*. Birthday girl, Phoebe, what did he get you for your birthday?'

What was she saying, wanting Adele out of the picture? I never wanted that despite the things I'd found out about her. Whatever she'd done, she was still a missing person! Why was Janice interested in Alan? Janice took a step closer the bloody blade glimmered in the light.

'Nothing,' I said.

'As if I'm going to believe that the birthday girl got nothing!' she said.

'He bought me dinner.'

'Nice. What else?'

She looked so much like me with that black wig.

'What else?' she insisted.

I glanced at Nash lying on the floor, blood oozing out of her body, not moving. She might have been dead already.

'Don't tell me he didn't give you the honour of receiving his cock, being the birthday girl and all. I've seen you come out of his place, so I assume it's a yes. You benefited more than I did.'

What was she talking about, benefited more than I did? Did Janice and Alan know each other before Adele introduced them?

'Oh yes, before you and Adele went batshit crazy over Alan, he and I had a fling. It was only brief. He was fresh out of a relationship. I was the rebound girl.'

It all came back to me; Alan had told me about a girl who was a rebound before Adele, and he didn't bother to tell anyone it was Janice? Did Adele know? No, I didn't think she did. I couldn't stand it; all those lies and secrets. My mind flashed back to the party Greg had invited me to, how annoyed Alan had looked when Janice and Hannah walked in.

'We were seeing each other for two months,' Janice went on. 'Then *bang,* he broke it off. It broke my heart. Then Adele announces she wanted to hook up with this fox named Alan. You can imagine the look on his face when he saw me with her. He didn't know we were friends. Now, you've tasted him too. He's exquisite, isn't he? But you're letting him win,' she said, her face turning dark. 'You know what the problem is with you? You let a man get between you and Adele and now she's gone.'

'Adele let men come between us because she can't keep her legs closed,' I said.

'Well, you didn't keep yours closed for long after she left. I was testing you both. He was more careful with you, given you're the one with the crush. Taking you to the house, meeting his mother, that should have been me, not *you!*' she shouted.

'Don't you think you should take this up with Alan, not with me?' I said. 'And you're doing this because of a man which makes you no different from Adele.'

'I will after I'm through with you.'

'Did you kill Dylan?' I asked.

'Ah, Dylan. If only you had seen the look on his face when he saw me standing at his door as I plunged a knife into him. He didn't see it coming. I'll do the same to Mr Cool next door.'

She lunged forward towards me, the blade sharp and bloody.

'Please,' I said.

She ran the knife to my chin, smearing my face with Nash's blood. The room smelt of death and dread. What am I going to do? How am I going to get myself out of this? She was going to kill me.

'It didn't have to be like this,' she said.

'It doesn't have to be,' I said.

'It's too late now.' She removed the black wig and her blonde hair fell over her shoulders.

'No, it's not…'

'Don't beg, Phoebe, it's not a good look. You and Adele were never meant to be friends, but she pitied you.'

My heart leapt into my mouth. The knife was on my throat, my eyes desperately searched for something, anything. There was nothing I could use as a weapon. But anything can be a weapon. Janice leaned closer to me, the blade cool against my skin. The pain came hot and fast.

Chapter Thirty-seven

The pain was unbearable. Blood, so much of it. I used my hands to push my body forward. I didn't know where I was going. Black spots clouded my vision. It was an instinct to get away. Footsteps came from behind me. Janice wasn't done with me, not until I was dead. She knelt beside me and turned me over, gripping my throat. My windpipe was crushed and my breathing became harder. I tried to fight her off using my hands, but I was too weak and the blackness was drowning me. A wave of exhaustion and pain washed over me. I couldn't fight her off. Janice squeezed harder and harder, using all the strength within her.

A force pulled Janice off me and I gasped for air and coughed. I heard protests. Through my distorted vision, I made out Alan, standing in the living room, his jaw clenched, his face dark, unreadable, cold and emotionless. He held Janice's hands behind her back. The knife skidded to the floor. She fought and kicked to set herself free. She was a trapped animal. I see it happen in slow motion. She freed herself but Alan grabbed her by the hair, yanking her back. Her scream pierced through the walls. She was like a rag doll in his arms. Alan pushed her and her head slammed against the edge of the coffee table and she fell limp on the floor.

There was silence as Alan stared at Janice's unmoving body. He rushed to me, taking off his jacket to apply pressure to the wound. There was a look of panic now.

'Jesus Christ, hold onto my jacket, okay?'

His voice faded, nausea and tiredness were taking over. He attended to Nash's wounds, cursing, and as he reached for the phone, the blackness overtook me.

There was a small hissing and a rhythmic beeping as my vision swam into focus. I was in a hospital room. The blinds were closed and there was someone else with me in the room, another patient. A blue blanket was thrown over me and my whole body was numb. I floated above the pain; it would come soon but for now, I would just float away from the agony and emotions and drift off.

I had been lucky. I have been told another centimetre and I could have died. Was I lucky? I wondered. I was operated on. Now the pain and emotions were close to me. Police officers came and went, asking me the same questions. I made sure I repeated the same thing. The stitches throbbed. Nash didn't die. Alan saved both of us. It went on like this, a stream of police officers between my visit from my parents and Tom.

I didn't know how long I had been in the hospital. I had dozed off and I woke up and Alan was there gazing at me, his eyes tender, loving almost. He was sitting on the chair by the side of the bed.

'I'm so happy you're okay,' he said.

Was I okay? Would I ever be?

He looked at his shoes. 'I didn't know, she... I met her several months ago. We started seeing each other on and off, then I broke it off...' he paused. 'She was the... rebound I told you about.'

'Janice is dead?'

He nodded. 'I should have known.'

I stared at him.

'Janice came to see me that afternoon and gave me this look; it was so strange.'

'What did she tell you?'

Alan rubbed his face with his hands. 'That I'm scum. I couldn't go on using women,' he made quotation marks on "using". He fell quiet, gazing at his shoes. 'The first time I saw Janice after I broke it off was at the party. I didn't know her and Adele were friends, it came as quite a surprise...'

'She killed... Dylan too.'

'I know.'

I tried to prop myself up on the pillow, but it was too painful. Alan stood and helped me.

'So, Adele is still…'

'Missing… yes,' he said.

Where was Adele? Why didn't she come back? I glanced at the window. The other patient snored.

'Did Adele know about you and Janice?' I asked. 'Did she know you two were seeing each other?'

'I didn't mention it. I don't think Janice did either, so no, I suppose she doesn't know.'

He said *doesn't* not *didn't*. Alan was still referring to Adele in the present tense. As if he still had hope. Was there hope? Was Adele out there? Had she heard about this? Did she know Janice was now gone too? The exhaustion swept over me, coming and going like a tide.

'Can we talk about something else?' I asked.

Alan smiled awkwardly. 'Sure, what do you want to talk about?'

'What are you up to?'

'I'm going back.'

'What do you mean?'

'Piano, but not solo, with someone else. I teamed up with a singer.'

I tried to smile, but the pain was sharp and angry.

'That's brilliant.'

'Thank you. Oh, I changed my number. I'll give it to you when you're out of here,' he said.

Alan leaned closer, ran his hand through my hair and kissed me on the lips.

'Get well soon, I miss you.'

Tom walked in then, and Alan and I glanced at him. Tom didn't look too happy to see Alan there. In his eyes, all that had happened was because of Alan, but it wasn't his fault. How could he have known?

Alan turned on his heel and I wanted to beg him to stay a little longer. Tom looked at me before he followed Alan outside. They were gone a while. Maybe he wanted to thank him for saving my life.

Alan never came to see me again.

I was released from hospital and Mum wanted me to stay with her. She didn't want me to return to the flat. Worried, it would bring back bad memories. I had bad memories either way, and I couldn't face Adele's mother when her daughter was still considered missing. Two people are dead because of this. It would have been four with me and Nash.

Mum wanted me to move out of the apartment and I agreed. All this time and not even a single word from Alan. He'd said he had changed his number but he had mine. Why wouldn't he get in touch with me? Panic surged through me.

After a week of being at home, in bed watching TV or reading, with the pain coming and going, I popped two painkillers and took a taxi to Alan's apartment. I rang the bell, but there was no answer. I stabbed the bell until my finger was sore. My stitches ached and burned. An old woman came out from the next-door apartment and squinted at me.

'What do you want?' she hissed. 'Can't you see no one is there! You woke me from my nap!'

'I'm very sorry, but does Alan Wiley still live here?' I asked her.

She blinked at me, confused. 'No, he moved out a month ago.'

A month! Moved where? Where did he go? My fears were coming alive, a blackness took over me, leaving me pained and injured.

'Do you know where he went?' I choked.

'No,' she said and shut the door.

A new pain rushed over me, making me weaker.

Adele had been lost, now Alan was lost too. Who does this? Who leaves without saying a word? Why didn't Alan tell me he planned to move elsewhere instead of telling me he missed me? Where did he go?

Three

Months

Later

Chapter Thirty-eight

I graduated from university in finance. It's all I could do to cope, bury my head in books and resume my plans. It kept me busy so I wouldn't think about the pain I felt, the betrayal that loomed over me. I found a job; something corporate, grey, and boring. A bookkeeper. I inputted invoices all day and sometimes I assist the other accountants in audits. This was a temporary job until I found something better. I looked around me and asked myself, was this what I studied for? To sit in an office, looking at screens and counting numbers for long hours of godforsaken days. It was neither impactful nor inspiring. We weren't scientists finding cures to life-threatening diseases. We were zombies. I joined the line of the undead in a soul-sucking job.

I moved out of the flat and into somewhere smaller than the previous one. A shoebox. But it was in London, and it was so glamorous to live there. Everything felt like fulfilling an obligation, a duty that must be done, doing something to feel useful. I went to work every day with a disheartening feeling. I looked at girls my age or younger than me and thought about what they had to go through, the men they were going to meet, how they were going to be let down, constantly, over and over, and do things they'd later regret. Not even a single word from Alan. It was like I was never in his life, like what we went through didn't happen. Like he didn't know me, like I never existed, like Adele never existed. The best way to cope was to turn your back on something and pretend it didn't happen, but it had *happened* and running wasn't the answer. There were so many unanswered questions. I needed closure. Alan was declared a hero for saving two lives, mine and a detective's and now he was gone. Was that why Alan told me he changed his number? He'd already decided by then? So, I went on joining the walking wounded.

I worked long hours; I didn't mind. I had nothing to welcome me in my cubical of a flat. No one to go home to. It was a coping mechanism, burying myself in work. My mum complained I was driving myself crazy. Who works eighty hours a week? It was all I had. Tom was busy planning the wedding and I despised it. Him being happy when I was rotting away.

I was assisting with the final touches of an audit when I went down to the canteen for a cup of coffee and a sandwich. I sat down at a table and there was a week-old newspaper. I flipped through the pages while I ate and there he was, on the engagements and weddings page. I had to look twice to make sure it was him. It was. *Allan Styles*. The picture was clear; him with his greasy hairstyle, and that smouldering, seductive gaze. He was lost, and now he was found. How in three months had he met someone and gone down on one knee to put the ring on her finger? The woman who stole him away was Emma Taylor, the daughter of an investment banker. She was a singer and I was transported back to the hospital. He'd said he was going back to the piano and working with a singer. Was it her? Had he already met her? How long had it been going on? Was he seeing her while...

But there was never him and me. It was just me and would always be. We were two people thrown together by terrible fate and somehow we managed—to what? I couldn't describe what we'd had apart from the fact he used me and I let him. That visit to the hospital wasn't because he wanted to see me, to see how I was, but his way to say goodbye. What a shitty thing to do. Alan was busy falling in love with this phoney while I had my body stitched and was in pain. I wanted to smash the canteen, tear it apart until there was nothing left of it, but the shock hit me so hard that silence took over.

I went to my shithole of a flat and cried until my body ached and heaved. Facing the days was unbearable, knowing Alan was out there, somewhere in his glamorous, pristine life while I was drowning in misery. I had my closure, after all, a fuck you in a newspaper in the engagements and wedding announcements section. How lovely. Alan didn't even consider what he had done. The damage and wreckage he had left behind to start fresh with someone else. Alan didn't do social media, but Emma did. His wife to be was accessible. They were going to get married in three months. A Christmas wedding.

Emma had curly red hair and green eyes with high sculpted cheekbones. She wasn't beautiful, even pretty. First the two blondes, Adele and Janice, then the raven-haired me, and now a red-haired Emma, testing them all. The full set. Alan the swine. There were photos of them together and a storm raged in my heart. It shook me to my deepest core, in places I didn't know existed within me. Was this the life he wanted for himself? Tea parties and Sunday lunches with both of their parents? This engagement seemed like a picture his mum wanted to paint. The two of them were going to perform at the Royal Albert Hall. The tickets were off the roof expensive, but all I did was work and save. A few hundred quid on a concert would not hurt me. Not for as important an event as this. I needed a front-row seat and I would get that front-row seat as if my life depended on it, I would bring my own chair if needs be, as long I'd be on the front row. Did he think he could move on and pretend nothing had happened? What about Adele? She was still gone. Had he thought about that? Did he ever think about her?

I didn't tell anyone I was going to see Alan perform. Not even Tom. What was the point?

'Maybe it's all for the best. Look at the chaos he brought along with him. Adele is still missing,' Tom had said.

Did Alan think of me and Adele when he lay in the dark as he smoked his cigarette? Whose face did he see when he pushed inside Emma; did Adele enter his thoughts? Did he think of Janice? Did I drift into his thoughts when he played the piano? He killed for me and he was forever stained with it. It would follow him wherever he went. Did Alan cry, knowing he had taken a life to save another? That my friend was still out there missing and the case was unsolved?

Adele was my best friend and yes, she was a shitty friend but she was my only friend and he took her away from me. He took her away from the moment he started dating her. How could he move on, turn his back on everything, when she was still out there? I had no one left. I was alone. I had nobody apart from Tom, but he too was getting married. Did Alan think he could live his happy ever after? But Alan had killed before. Although I had no proof of this, he might have killed Perry White, the journalist who didn't review him as a musician but made snarky remarks about his person. It must have gotten to Alan, the outrage, who was that fat fuck to criticize him anyway. He was ugly and bitter because once he wanted to be a musician, but failed and was taking it out on other musicians who'd "made it". Alan was handsome, talented, and people worshipped the ground he walked on. He was loved but capable of doing horrible things, as we all can. No one would believe me that lovely Alan paid Perry a visit, and set up the murder as a sex game gone wrong but this was my theory.

If Alan had no intention to stay, why had he saved my life? To leave me to suffer like this? I might as well be dead. I was already dead. I was empty. I was just a blank space drifting along; I had no meaning. No substance. I was hollow. I was the abyss.

The clapping swam around the room and the crowds stood; there were cheers and whistles. Alan flashed a million-dollar smile and waved at the crowd. For someone who hated being up there on that stage, he appreciated his admirers. There was another cheer, as if he were a hero that had saved the day. Alan, however, *was* the virtuoso, the young maestro, the magician behind the piano.

I waited outside at the back area of the hall. Two sleek black BMWs were waiting outside. A small crowd of fans gathered to get pictures and autographs from their heroes. The door opened and Emma came out and someone handed her roses and others posed with their phones to snap a photo of their idol. So, it would go up on fucking Facebook to show off. Alan came out a few minutes later, wearing a black shirt and a leather jacket and black jeans. I noticed his hair was different, still with the James Dean cool but now much lighter in colour. It looked almost dark blond. He stopped and smiled at the girl who was talking to him. I could see he hated this part but played along. Emma got in the car and Alan turned. I didn't know what made him look in my direction, but I was glad he did. I was his only audience now, perhaps I always was. I was only admiring him from afar and he was unreachable. Always had been. He'd deliberately made himself that way.

I was the mouse and he was the cat. I've always been the mouse. What was a mouse when it had teeth? A cassowary disguised as a peacock. His eyes went wide, but I saw no horror in them. Alan had been found once more, but Adele was still lost.

You can buy the follow up Hide and Seek book 2 to find what really had happened to Adele.

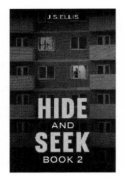

She went missing but someone doesn't want her to be found.

Hope is waning with Phoebe no closer to finding her best friend, Adele. Her suspicions involving her neighbor, Alan, have been cleared, leaving her no other hunches to pursue.

Until the letter arrives.

A message, written in Adele's hand, paints a picture of a side of her friend's life Phoebe never knew. Renewed with optimism that she is still alive, Phoebe launches back into the investigation. Among the pages of Adele's communications Phoebe finds evidence pointing to an unlikely suspect...

And yet another connection to Alan.

He seemed so concerned about the investigation, wanting to help in any way he could.

Was the man next door a genuine ally? Or working to protect the real culprit? Would Phoebe be able to find Adele?

Note from The Author

If you enjoy what I write, you can help this little writer out by writing a review on Amazon or Goodreads or any platform of your choice. Reviews are the lifeline for authors and readers trust other readers. If you use social media, spread the word. It will be wonderful to have my book listed with others you have enjoyed.

You can leave a review.

Love,

J.S Ellis xx

You can sign up for my newsletter, and keep updated with new releases, offers, updates and giveaways.

https://joannewritesbooks.com

If you enjoyed this book you might also enjoy:
The Rich Man

 Her boyfriend vanished, but moving on could be murder...

Acey left without a word, leaving Elena alone to pick up the pieces of her broken heart. Determined not to be crushed by his betrayal, she forces herself to get over him.

Never did she fathom the unspeakable darkness closing in...

Sinclair Diamond breezes into her life like an answered prayer. Handsome. Wealthy. Charming. As he lovingly dotes on her, Elena finds herself falling for him.

But Sinclair has unspeakable secrets all his own.

Men in black suits trailing them. Shady business dealings. The odd chain of events surrounding his first wife's death. The more Elena learns about Sinclair, the more her apprehension builds. Yet when a ghost from her past reappears, Elena is forced to face a startling truth that could cost her everything.

Can she escape the web of deceit tightening around her? Or will she be the next to mysteriously disappear?

Theodore: The Neighbour's Cat

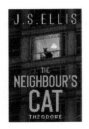

My roommate is a serial killer.

And I have been powerless to stop him because I... am a cat.

Don't get me wrong, Dean has never been cruel to me. He provides me with shelter, toys, and plenty of affection. But I have seen his dark side, his brutal treatment of women, and I can't bear to watch anyone else get hurt.

Jane from next door is attractive for a human, not to mention being incredibly kind. That kindness may get her killed. I've seen how Dean looks at her, I know what he's plotting. In his mind, she's his for the taking. I wasn't able to save the others, but I'm not ready to give up. One way or another, I have to figure out how to communicate to Jane that she's in danger.

Can I find a way to warn her in time? Or will she become just another name on his growing list of victims?

The Secret She Kept: She's dead. Why would she lie?

Days before her murder, Anthony's friend, Lottie, lent him her laptop. Curiosity getting the best of him, he clicks on a file and finds videos recorded by her in the year leading up to her death. Within those recordings, she exposes dark secrets someone will kill to keep hidden, and Lottie's toxic relationship with Anthony's long-time friend, Davian.

When Anthony's childhood friend, Davian is placed under arrest for the murder, Anthony refuses to believe he could do such a thing but Lottie was infatuated by Davian. More damning evidence piles up, Anthony wonders if it's possible a man he's known for most of his life has kept a sinister side of himself hidden.

Now, Anthony faces an impossible choice; turn the laptop over to the police and risk being accused of hindering the investigation, or try to solve the case himself. Lottie gave him the computer for a reason. There was something there she wanted him to see. Can he put the pieces of the puzzle together in time to uncover the killer?

In Her Words: One night. One woman. One Man. One Mystery.

While she seems to have it all, Sophie Knight is looking for more. When gorgeous and carefree Michael Frisk walks into her life, he offers the excitement and passion she desires.

Sophie is willing to risk everything she has. After all, she is used to concealing things from her husband—like her alcoholism, her unhappiness. But soon she has more to hide. She wakes up one morning in an alcoholic haze and finds bruises on her body, but has no recollection of what happened to her. Was she raped?

When unsettling notes and mysterious phone calls start, Sophie wonders whom she should turn to. Is Michael the cause of the frightening things happening in her life, or is he the answer to her problems?

The Confidant

 Secrets have deadly consequences.

A part of him knew she was always lying, but he could change that. He could change her.

When charismatic Zoë first sits in Jason's salon chair, he can immediately tell they have a connection. Who wouldn't? She was smart, witty, and incredibly funny, everything someone could want in a budding friendship. But soon, Jason learns there is more to Zoë than meets the eye.

When lies are uncovered and secrets exposed, Jason must decide just how far he's willing to go in the name of friendship.

How far should he go to uncover the truth? If he digs too deep, could Jason lose the very person he's trying to keep?

When it all comes crashing to the light, and someone's

very life hangs in the balance, will he regret what he's done? Or will Jason wish he had only done more?

Scan the code to buy the books

About the author.

J.S Ellis is a thriller author. She lives in Malta with her husband and their furbabies, Eloise and Theo. When she's not writing or reading, she's either cooking, eating cheese and chocolate, or listening to good music and enjoying a glass of wine or two.

Website https://joannewritesbooks.com

Facebook https://www.facebook.com/authorJ.SEllis/

Instagram @ author_j.sellis

Goodreads http://bit.ly/2P8a9xx

Pinterest: https://bit.ly/3iqBvrU

Amazon: https://amzn.to/30rbKSq

Bingebooks: https://bingebooks.com/author/j-s-ellis

Bookbub: https://www.bookbub.com/authors/j-s-ellis

Made in the USA
Monee, IL
12 August 2023

40893332R00166